"I just want to  Shayn

And so he did, pressing his hot mouth down on hers, forcing his tongue between her parted lips. Her body exploded with heat. She opened her mouth to him, letting his tongue go deeper, and sighing with the pleasure of it. It was a hot and desperate kiss, far too inappropriate for public, but Shayna didn't care. All she wanted right now was to indulge in this flirtation to the fullest. She kissed Donovan wantonly, kissed him as though he was the man she was supposed to be with on her honeymoon.

As his lips caressed hers, his fingers skimmed the side of one of her breasts. Shayna mewled, wishing he could touch the part of her that craved his fingers, but knowing he couldn't.

He moved with her through the water to the side, where he gently leaned Shayna's body against a large rock. Her legs were still wrapped around him, and as he kissed her senseless, he held her more tightly, and she clung to him.

Books by Kayla Perrin

Kimani Romance

Island Fantasy #173

KAYLA PERRIN

has been writing since the age of thirteen and once entertained the idea of becoming a teacher. Instead, she has become a *USA TODAY* and *Essence* bestselling author of dozens of mainstream and romance novels, and has been recognized for her talent, including twice winning Romance Writers of America's Top Ten Favorite Books of the Year Award. She has also won the Career Achievement Award for multicultural romance from *RT Book Reviews*. Kayla lives with her daughter in Ontario, Canada. Visit Kayla at www.KaylaPerrin.com.

ISLAND
Fantasy

USA TODAY BESTSELLING AUTHOR
KAYLA PERRIN

KIMANI™
ROMANCE

This book is for all of my family in Jamaica—my aunts, uncles and many cousins in the Perrin and the McKenzie family tree. I love each and every one of you!

And it's also for Agri Brady and the other friends I made at the Gran Bahia Principe hotel in Runaway Bay, Jamaica. Thank you for making my stay at your beautiful hotel simply wonderful. Your friendship and hospitality made the difference! I can't wait to go back!

 KIMANI PRESS™

Recycling programs for this product may not exist in your area.

ISBN-13: 978-0-373-86148-4

ISLAND FANTASY

Copyright © 2010 by Kayla Perrin

www.kimanipress.com

Printed in U.S.A.

Dear Reader,

Lately I've had many letters from my fans, asking me when I'm going to write another romance novel. I've dipped my hand in other pots, writing some suspense, erotica and general women's fiction, but romance is where I started, and romance is still in my heart.

So for those of you who have been waiting for another one of my romances, for those who enjoy reading all of my stories, and for those who might be reading one of my books for the first time, I'm very pleased to have *Island Fantasy* to share with you.

Many of us—if not all—have experienced heartbreak at some point in our lives. Many of us have experienced betrayal. What if you experienced a crushing betrayal on the night of your wedding? Would you get married anyway, hoping that your fiancé simply had prewedding jitters and that once he said "I do" all would be fine? Or would you have the courage—in front of all of your wedding guests— to say that you deserve better?

My heroine, Shayna Kenyon, has the courage to call off the wedding, knowing that a man who would betray her the night of her wedding isn't a man who deserves her heart. It's not an easy thing to do, but doing the right thing isn't always easy. I wrote Shayna's story to show a woman's courage in the eleventh hour. To show that even if you're about to say "I do" and suddenly realize it's not right, it's not too late to say "I don't."

I really enjoyed writing Shayna and Donovan's love story. I hope you enjoy their quest for true love on the beautiful and sultry island of Jamaica. And be sure to look for Brianne's story—Shayna's sister—in my next Kimani Romance.

And now, indulge your *Island Fantasy*.

Kayla

Chapter 1

Shayna Kenyon didn't consider herself a vengeful person. Revenge was not her style. In life, she had been able to turn the other cheek when people had wronged her. Been able to move forward and leave any ugliness in the past.

But last night… A flash of what she'd witnessed with her own two eyes entered her brain, causing her stomach to twist harshly. She couldn't very well move forward from Vince's betrayal in the same easy fashion she had moved forward when necessary in the past.

Especially not today.

Today… Oh, Lord help her.

The depth of Vince's betrayal burned deep in her soul. And the timing of it couldn't have been worse.

Shayna inhaled a deep, shaky breath. Her eyes misted, but she held back her tears. She had to do what she was about to do. There was no other choice.

"Baby, it's okay," her father said and held her arm a little closer to his side. "There's no need to cry. You're marrying a man who adores you, and if I do say so myself, you look incredible. You're my daughter, yes, but I mean it when I say this—you're the most beautiful bride I've ever seen. Other than your mother," he added with a smile. "This is your day. Enjoy it."

Enjoy it, Shayna thought sourly. She hadn't enjoyed anything since last night—and she had the puffy eyes to prove it. She'd told her parents that she'd been too excited to sleep, which wasn't the truth. She'd been too devastated to truly rest. All night, she had lain awake, alternately crying and contemplating what to do.

Her decision—approved by her sister—was the only thing giving her the power to walk down the aisle. The fact that there would be some satisfaction in what was coming next. It was the only reason she'd gotten all dressed up and spent two hours getting her hair and makeup done. To see the look on Vince's face when she let him—and all the guests in attendance—know that she knew.

The last of Shayna's five bridesmaids took her place on the podium. After a few beats of silence, the local singer she and Vince had hired began her rendition of "Here I Am" by Beyoncé and Eric Benét. Shayna and Vince had opted for something more contemporary as opposed to the traditional organ music signaling the bride's walk down the aisle.

Shayna swallowed, tears falling from her eyes even though she didn't want them to. Her father pulled the handkerchief from his breast pocket and dabbed at her cheeks.

"Come on, baby," he urged. "Everyone's waiting."

Shayna hesitated a beat, suddenly unsure. But even her sister had encouraged her to do what she was about to do next. "Do what you need to do," her younger sister, Brianne, had told her. "As far as I'm concerned, Vince deserves much worse than public humiliation."

The singer continued the soulful love ballad, and Shayna

knew she should start moving. Through the church's back door windows, she could see everyone on their feet, waiting for her to take her final walk as a single woman.

The doors opened. She began to move. She was nervous and devastated, and yet she tried to force a smile. Given her state of mind, she wasn't sure she accomplished her goal.

All around her, people were grinning. Some grinning and crying. This was a wonderful occasion. One she'd waited thirty-two years for. Her family was ecstatic that she'd found the kind of love that lasted a lifetime.

Shayna knew better, and soon everyone else would, too.

While walking down the aisle, Shayna hadn't allowed herself to look directly at Vince, afraid she would fall apart. But as she neared him, she did. Her stomach lurched with disgust when she saw the tears streaming down his face.

Tears of joy, or tears of shame?

The tears of shame would come soon—that much she was sure of.

Near the pulpit, her father stopped, faced her and dabbed at his own tears before kissing her cheek. "I love you, baby," he said.

"I love you, too," Shayna said, her voice a whisper.

She hoped her father wouldn't be upset with her ruse, but she knew his wrath would be for Vince. Vince, who'd behaved like the son her father had never had.

How could you? Shayna wondered, and then took the two steps onto the podium to join her groom.

The singer finished her song. Vince took Shayna's hands in his, his eyes lighting up with warmth.

"Baby, you look amazing," he told her, and Shayna wanted to yank her hands from his grip. She was past the devastation, at least temporarily, and was going on pure anger.

"Dearly beloved," the minister intoned. "We are gathered here today—"

"Excuse me," Shayna interrupted, her stomach fluttering. She had known she would speak, but she hadn't expected it to be just then. But she couldn't fake it a moment longer. Couldn't stand the sight of Vince acting like the happy fiancé. "I—I need to say something."

The minister looked confused. So did Vince.

But when neither objected, Shayna forged ahead, meeting her fiancé's tear-filled eyes. "Actually, I have a question for you, *sweetheart*." She added the last word with much exaggeration.

"What, baby?" Vince asked, looking and sounding concerned. "What is it?"

Part of her wanted to turn and run down the aisle. That would be easier than confronting Vince publicly. And yet, she'd made up her mind. Difficult or not, she was going to do what she'd planned.

"Do you love me, Vince?" Shayna asked. "Love me enough that you believe you're making the right decision by marrying me?"

A hum of surprise sounded in the crowd. People were curious now, perhaps some realizing that something wasn't right.

"Of course I do," Vince responded. He squeezed Shayna's hands tighter and chuckled softly in relief, his tone saying he felt his bride was suffering from last-minute jitters. "You know I love you more than anything, baby. You're the one I want to grow old with. Have children with. Spend the rest of my life with."

There were some, "Awwws," and a few people even clapped—that's how perfect Vince's answer had been.

"Shall I continue?" the minister asked. The warm smile on his face said he also believed that Shayna had simply needed reassuring.

Shayna faced the minister. A beat passed. Then she said, "Just one more question."

Silence filled the church, so much so that the buzzing of a fly could be heard. Shayna swallowed the lump in her throat so that she could find her voice, aware that everyone was waiting to hear what she had to say.

She straightened her shoulders and said, "You love me."

"Of course."

"You love me so much you ended up in your car after your bachelor party, *making out with a stripper!*"

Startled gasps erupted in the pews.

"Baby," Vince said. He tried to chuckle, but the sound was hollow. "A—a stripper? W-what?"

Shayna pulled her hands from the man she was grateful not to be marrying. "Don't you dare try to lie, Vince. I saw you with my own eyes! You were parked right outside the private hall you rented, you jerk. I saw you leave the building with her. I saw you go to your car with her. And I saw what happened after that, too."

Vince said nothing, but Shayna saw the panic in his widened eyes. The disbelief that she could possibly know what he'd done.

Shayna glanced to her left, at her sister, who was her maid of honor. Brianne nodded her encouragement.

"And *baby*," Shayna went on, slowly and clearly, "if that's your definition of love, then I'll pass on the whole marrying you thing, thank you very much."

Vince's mouth fell open, but he was too startled to speak. A buzz of surprised chatter instantly filled the church. The groomsmen and bridesmaids all stared at Shayna, stunned looks on their faces. Shayna would answer their questions—but not yet.

Running on adrenaline, Shayna gathered her wide organza

skirt in her hands and turned as swiftly as she could. She hustled back down the aisle, aware that all eyes were on her.

She knew she would cry later, but for that moment, as she neared the back doors of the church, she smiled.

Vince Danbury may have had a scandalously good time last night, but Shayna had just had the last laugh.

Chapter 2

"**You're still going on your honeymoon?**" Brianne asked Shayna later that afternoon, the look on her face saying she thought her sister was crazy.

"I'm not going on my *honeymoon*," Shayna clarified. She was running her fingers through her shoulder-length hair, trying to loosen the tight spiral curls the hairdresser had done such a great job of creating for her wedding. "A honeymoon requires two people who just tied the knot."

"You know what I mean," Brianne said. "You still plan to go to Jamaica tomorrow—the trip that was *supposed* to be your honeymoon?"

"Seven days in Jamaica? Of course I'm going."

Brianne placed her hands on her hips as she stared at Shayna, who sat on the edge of Brianne's bed. "You're serious."

Shayna didn't respond. Instead, her eyes traveled over her sister—from the white orchid adorning her short black hair to the pale yellow maid of honor dress. "Do me a favor, sis?

Take that dress off, please?" Her wedding dress had been the first thing Shayna had taken off when she'd gotten to her parents' house, slipping into a pair of her sister's shorts and a T-shirt. "I really don't want any reminders of Vince."

"Oh." Brianne smoothed her hands over the dress. "Right." She reached behind her to drag down the zipper. "Such a shame I didn't get to wear this all day. After all that weight I lost for your wedding…"

Her sister did look fabulous. At the beginning of the year, she'd started a diet and rigorous workout routine to get in better shape for Shayna's wedding. She'd lost thirty-five pounds.

Brianne walked toward the closet, shimmying the dress off her shoulders. She found a red sundress with a formfitting halter neck and slipped into that.

Brianne twirled around, facing Shayna again in the casual dress. "Better?"

Shayna nodded. "Yes. Except for the flower."

Brianne pulled the flower from her hair and tossed it onto her dresser. "Now, back to your trip—"

"Yes, I'm going."

"But you're grieving," Brianne protested. "This isn't the time to go on a trip alone."

"Why not?"

"Because you hate even going to a movie alone," Brianne pointed out. "I can't see you going on a trip by yourself."

"Well, I am."

The look Brianne flashed her sister was full of doubt. She thought Shayna was bluffing.

"I'm a big girl," Shayna went on. "I'm entitled."

"I know, but—"

"But what? You think I'm going to do something crazy?"

"Maybe you will," Brianne said, but her tone quavered, indicating she didn't believe her sister would do anything out of character. "Maybe you'll end up marrying the first man who hits on you."

Shayna laughed out loud at that.

"Don't laugh. Remember that happened to my friend Gloria's friend's sister."

Shayna scowled at Brianne. "That was in Vegas, and she was drunk and on the rebound."

"You're on the rebound."

"Rebound? Already?" Shayna's heart spasmed, but somehow, she found the strength to force a laugh. "Right now I should be at the park, taking perfect wedding photos with that expensive photographer Daddy hired. Instead..." Her voice trailed off. She couldn't go on, or she would cry. "Bree, the way I feel right now, if I never see another man, it'll be too soon. Trust me."

Brianne took a seat beside Shayna on the bed. "Shay, I'm so sorry. Part of me wishes I'd never suggested we drive by that hall to see what the groomsmen were up to."

"And if we hadn't, I'd be married right now—not knowing that my husband was a dirty cheating jerk." The anger helped Shayna hold back any tears. "No, I'm glad you suggested it. Everything happens for a reason, and in this case, it was to spare me the pain of marrying the wrong man." Shayna was amazed at how calmly and rationally she was dealing with the situation, but she truly believed that nothing good came of fretting over something she couldn't control. "I don't want to be married for the sake of being married. I need to be with a man who loves and adores me enough not to sleep with some stripper he just met. To know—even if he was drunk—that no other woman could ever tempt him away from the woman who's in his heart."

Brianne shook her head, the look on her face suddenly venomous. "I still can't believe Vince could do that. If we hadn't witnessed it, I never would have believed him capable of that kind of betrayal."

"Me neither," Shayna said softly. "And the night before our wedding? That's the reason I need to go away. I can't be around here, see all the places we liked to go to. I can't deal with the calls from everyone. I'm holding it together now, but I know at some point I'm going to fall apart."

"Which is why you need to be with your family. People who love you."

Shayna smiled, loving her sister for caring so much, though if the situation were reversed, Shayna would be saying the same thing to Brianne. They were eighteen months apart, but as close as twins. They'd been there for each other through every triumph and tragedy in each other's lives.

Like when Brianne had lost her boyfriend, Carter. Three years ago, Carter had vanished while hiking in the Rockies. After weeks of searching for him and finding only his backpack, the authorities came to the conclusion that he'd likely died of exposure, and that coyotes or other wildlife must have eaten his remains. It had been the worst time of Brianne's life—after which she'd turned to food for comfort. Shayna had been there for her sister through the entire harrowing ordeal.

"I know how much you love me," Shayna said, smiling softly. "And I appreciate you caring for me. But I need some time for myself. Time to reflect on everything. Time to lie in bed and do nothing if I don't want to. Time to sit on the beach and read all those books I thought I'd never have time to read. Time to just…get away from it all."

"You're sure?" Brianne asked.

"Yes, I'm sure," Shayna said, feigning a confidence she didn't feel. "'Still I rise,'" she went on, quoting Maya Angelou. "I'm a strong black woman. This is a setback in my life, but it won't keep me down. And hey, the trip is paid for. I'm pretty certain Vince won't be going. But I'll gain some small measure of satisfaction knowing that his money will fund my seven days in paradise."

"Serves the idiot right," Brianne said.

Shayna hugged her sister, long and hard, then got to her feet. "I'd love to stay and chat, but I've got to go home and pack."

That wasn't entirely true. Shayna was mostly packed already, and her flight wasn't until the next afternoon. But she was ready to be alone.

"Besides," Shayna continued, "the limo driver's not going to want to wait all day." He'd driven her to the church, and he'd driven her back to her parents' place. It was a painful reminder of the wedding that never was, but the car had been paid for. Might as well utilize it.

"Let me at least walk you to the door."

Shayna caught her reflection in Brianne's dresser mirror. Her makeup was exquisite—and totally illogical given the oversize T-shirt she was wearing. She would look even more out of place when she got into the limo like this, but she needed to get home.

She and Brianne headed out of the bedroom and downstairs to the front door of their parents' home. Shayna had already had time with her parents and Vince's, time to explain in more detail what had happened last night with Vince and why she wouldn't be marrying him. Now, all four parents had gone off to speak with Vince, most likely to try and talk some sense into his senseless brain. It didn't matter what they said—Shayna wouldn't forgive him, and there would be no rescheduled wedding date.

When Shayna and Brianne got to the front door, Brianne suddenly said, "If you want, I can see if I can call in sick to work and put the trip on my credit card so I can go with you."

Shayna wrapped her arms around Brianne and hugged her. Hugged her until she felt emotion clog her throat. "I love you for caring," Shayna said. "I really do. But this week…I need it for myself. If I stay here, Mom is going to cry all week, depress me with her 'I can't believe Vince would do this to you' talks. No one is going to be able to look at me without pity—not even you—and I don't want that. I already feel bad enough. I need this time—time to digest what's happened and pull myself together." Emotion finally got the better of her, and a sob escaped Shayna's throat while a tear rolled down her cheek.

"Oh, sweetie," Brianne crooned, rubbing Shayna's arms. "This is why I don't want you to be alone."

"I can't believe Vince did this to me," Shayna said, trying to keep herself from completely falling apart. "How could he destroy everything?"

"I know. No one expected him to betray you like this, least of all me."

"If he calls again, tell him I'm in an undisclosed location and can't be reached. I have nothing to say to him. That's another reason I want to be in Jamaica. He won't be able to drop by and see me. Won't be able to try and beg me to forgive him. I think I'd rather be in Timbuktu than Jamaica—as far away from Buffalo as possible—but Jamaica will have to do."

"I can't talk you out of it?" Brianne asked.

"Please don't worry about me. I'm going to be at a five-star resort. Nothing bad is going to happen to me. And I'll call you, every day if you want."

"All right," Brianne said. "You're a big girl. If you want to go on a trip alone, that's your right."

"I love you," Shayna said.

"I love you, too, sis."

Shayna gave her sister one last hug, then opened the front door. And when she did, the blood froze in her veins.

Vince was standing there.

A full five seconds passed with neither of them speaking, only staring at each other. Shayna was too startled to speak or even move.

"Shayna." Vince broke the silence. His voice was full of pain and perhaps also regret.

Shayna's eyes darted beyond Vince to her parents and then back to Vince. All of them looked distressed. And of course they were. The day that had begun with so much hope had ended in the worst possible way.

And it was all Vince's fault.

If not for their parents, Shayna was tempted to give Vince a piece of her mind and stalk off. Instead, she held herself together.

"Shayna, can we talk?"

Shayna swallowed. Her throat was suddenly dry, but she managed to find her voice. "There's nothing to say."

Mrs. Danbury stepped forward. The woman's eyes were red, as though she'd been crying. "Shayna, I know you're angry, and you have every right to be, but what Vince has to say…it might help."

So Vince had told his and her parents a pack of lies. Something that had them believing he was worthy of a second chance?

"Hear him out," Shayna's mother said. "No matter what happens, at some point you're going to have to talk."

Shayna gritted her teeth. As much as she didn't want to acknowledge it, her mother was right. At some point she and Vince *would* have to talk, settle everything. Thank God Shayna hadn't given up her apartment yet, because now she would not be moving into Vince's house as planned. She only hoped the landlord didn't have a rental agreement in place for when her lease was up in a month.

"All right," Shayna said. "If you want to talk, let's talk."

Vince's shoulders sagged with relief. He was still wearing his tux, though it was unbuttoned at the collar and the tie was loose. His dark, handsome face was drawn. "Thank you."

Don't thank me, Shayna thought. *No matter what you say, it's over.* Unless he told her that he'd been drugged and taken advantage of and had the toxicology reports to prove it—but that kind of story line only happened on soap operas.

"Let's go to the back patio," Shayna said flatly. "We can have some privacy there."

Shayna led the way, holding her head high, though it felt like her insides were being churned in a blender. She opened the back door and stepped onto the patio then took a seat at the small table. As Vince took a seat beside her, Shayna spoke. "I'm not sure what you think you can say that will excuse what you did."

"I'm sorry, baby. You have no clue how bad I feel."

"Not nearly as bad as I feel."

"It was a mistake," Vince went on. "A stupid, stupid mistake. Baby, I'm begging you—please forgive me. Forgive me, and I will spend the rest of my life proving to you that I'm worthy of you."

Shayna could hardly stand being this close to Vince. Part of her wished that a bolt of lightning would suddenly strike him dead. But what she really wanted was to end things once and for all and move on.

"I've got boxes at your place," she said. "Can you arrange to have them sent to my parents' house? It'll be less messy that way."

Vince looked crushed. She hadn't said what he'd wanted to hear. "Baby—"

"And please—stop calling me baby. You no longer have the right."

"I was drunk, Shayna. Do you really think I would have touched that woman if I were sober?"

"That's your excuse?"

"I know it's lame, but it's the truth."

"So any time in the future when you get drunk, you can't be trusted to be faithful."

"That's not what I'm saying."

"And what about all the women who hit on you in your practice? Or have you already crossed the line with some of your patients?"

"Shayna, stop it. You know that's not true."

"Do I? Because I never would have thought you capable of…of what you did." Shayna had to look away, because looking at Vince hurt too much. The beautiful foliage and flowers of the garden her mother had worked hard to cultivate over the years didn't bring her the sense of peace it normally did.

How could anything bring her peace right now?

Shayna flinched when she felt Vince's warm hand on hers. The gentle touch almost brought out her tears. He had ruined everything, destroyed their dreams.

"Baby." Vince sighed wearily. "I know you might not believe what I'm about to say next, but it's true. Look at me, please."

A beat passed, then Shayna raised her eyes to his.

"When I was in my car with that woman…I was so drunk, so damn out of it that I thought…" Vince paused. Swallowed. Gave Shayna a heartfelt look that on other occasions would have tugged at her heartstrings. And then he dropped his bombshell. "I was so drunk, I thought that it was you in the car with me."

It wasn't so much a bombshell as a slap in the face. An

insult to her intelligence. Was Vince actually saying…? Shayna stared at him, gauging just how serious he was.

The man was serious.

Seriously full of it.

"You're saying you thought that stripper was *me?*" Shayna asked, for clarification.

"I told you it would sound crazy, but yes, baby. That's the only reason I did anything with her. Because I thought she was you."

And just like that, Shayna was over him. Irrevocably. So much so that she actually laughed.

"Oh, Vince." She shook her head as she chuckled. "You know, I thought that between me and my friends I'd heard every line a man uses when he's caught cheating. But that—oh, man. That one takes the prize."

Vince's face fell. He looked surprised that Shayna didn't believe him.

No, he looked crushed.

Shayna pushed her chair back and stood. "I can see how you couldn't tell us apart—with our breast sizes being so similar."

Shayna snorted. The stripper's breasts had been so huge, she and her sister had marveled that the woman could walk. Which only made Vince's lie all the more lame.

"Plus her long red hair and white skin," Shayna continued. "So similar to my brown skin and black hair."

"I know it sounds crazy, but it's—"

"Have the boxes with my stuff delivered here as soon as possible," Shayna told Vince before she walked away. "Oh— and one more thing." She pulled the beautiful engagement ring he'd given her off her finger and plopped it onto the glass table in front of him. "Give this to the next woman fool enough to believe you're Mr. Right."

Then Shayna walked away, leaving a stunned Vince sitting

at her parents' patio table. "It's over," she announced to her and Vince's parents as she strolled through the living room, not even breaking stride. "I'm going home now."

No one tried to stop her. They obviously saw her resolve and knew not to test it.

If they'd held out any hope of a reconciliation, they had to know now that that would never happen.

Chapter 3

People stared at Shayna as she got out of the limo in front of her building. Of course they did. They all had to be wondering why a girl with great hair and makeup but dressed in casual clothes was getting out of a Hummer limo—alone. Especially one that had clearly been decked out for a wedding. Shayna had ripped off the "Just Married" sign at the back of the limo, but tissue-paper flowers and streamers still adorned the sides and front.

Shayna didn't meet any of the curious gazes. She just hustled into her building and up to her apartment. Once there, she turned off her cell phone and yanked the plugs of her two home phones out of the wall. She knew her parents and others would be calling, but she didn't want to talk to any of them. She stripped off her clothes and took a hot bubble bath, surprised that she no longer felt like crying.

Somehow, she had been truly able to put Vince behind her, and she had him to thank for that. If he'd stuck to apologizing profusely, Shayna might still feel some sadness over the end of their relationship. But that bald-faced lie about thinking he was with *her*...Vince simply didn't deserve her tears.

Later that night, after she had repacked her suitcase to include a myriad of books she would now get the chance to read, Shayna called her parents. She got pretty much the same protest from her mother about going to Jamaica alone that she'd gotten from her sister. Her mother didn't want Shayna alone during this difficult time. She wanted her eldest daughter surrounded by supportive family. Shayna assured her mother that she'd be fine and needed this time to herself.

"You're sure I can't change your mind?" Shayna's mother asked.

"I'll be fine, Mom. I'll call every day."

A beat passed. "Vince says you're mistaken," her mother said softly. "That what you saw was him trying to fight off that woman in the car. Granted, he shouldn't have allowed her in the car in the first place—"

"Funny," Shayna said, interrupting her mother. "Because he told me that he thought that stripper was *me*." Shayna let the words settle over her mother. "He's lying, Mom. Trying any story that will stick."

"He says he loves you, dear. With all his heart. He's so torn up over what's happened."

And Shayna's mother was torn up over the fact that her daughter wouldn't be marrying a doctor. Her dream had come true when Shayna had started dating Vince, whom she'd met by chance at a coffee shop when she'd been there working on her latest historical romance novel. And Shayna thought her dream of finding her real-life perfect hero had come true, as well.

Clearly, she'd been mistaken.

"You don't actually think I should forgive him?" Shayna asked her mother.

"No," Alice Kenyon said softly. "It's just…such a disappointment."

"I know it is. But the fact remains that Vince betrayed me. The night before our wedding. Nothing he says will ever explain away what he did. I would have far more respect for him if he could admit what he'd done, take ownership of his very bad behavior."

"All right, sweetheart. You go on your trip alone if you need to. But be careful. Take care of yourself."

"Like I told Brianne, I'm going to a five-star resort in Jamaica. I'll be in good hands, so please don't worry. I love you, Mom."

"I love you, too."

Shayna ended the call with her mother, finished packing the last of her things for her trip and headed to bed in her apartment—all too aware that it was a far cry from the posh honeymoon suite she and Vince had booked for the night.

About five hours later, Shayna was up in the middle of the night and driving to Toronto, where she and Vince were scheduled to fly to Jamaica on a charter plane.

She turned the radio on as she drove, hoping music would block out her thoughts. But within minutes, she was no longer focusing on the lyrics of Kanye West, but the reality that the last thirty hours hadn't been an awful dream.

Shayna had often taken playful ribbing from her friends about her single status. Especially when she'd hit thirty and still hadn't found her true love. They had teased her about the fact that she could come up with the best heroes in her novels, yet couldn't find one in her real life.

"Writing the perfect hero has taught me that the last thing I want to do is settle," Shayna always explained. It had become her mantra.

Shortly before her thirty-first birthday, she'd met Vince. And her life had changed. He was successful. Charming. Attractive. Finally, the man she'd been waiting for had come into her life.

Was he always a cheater? Shayna wondered. *Or did alcohol truly make him lose his mind on Friday night?*

A moment after the question popped into her mind, Shayna knew that it didn't matter. If he'd always been a cheater, then good riddance. If the alcohol had clouded his morality, then good riddance.

Gripping the steering wheel, she drew in a deep, calming breath. But she felt anything but calm. She felt anxious and hurt and relieved all in one.

Which was to be expected. Her mind might know better, but her heart was still reeling from shock.

She hoped that after a week in Jamaica she could return home with her mind, body and spirit refreshed, able to truly consider Vince a part of her past. Because it wasn't so much Vince she was grieving now as the loss of the dreams she'd had about her future with him.

She'd told herself that she wouldn't shed another tear over Vince. If he could so easily sleep with one of the strippers from the bachelor party in the backseat of his car on the night before their wedding, then he wasn't worth her tears. Yes, the life she'd been planning and hoping for had been taken away from her in the blink of an eye, but it was far better that Vince betrayed her now, before they said their I do's. Shayna's good friend, Christine, was still reeling from her husband's decision to leave her for another woman, and after six years of marriage, Christine was now a single mother.

No, if Vince was going to cheat, this was the time.

But as much as Shayna knew she needed to move on, she still felt pain deep in her soul. She wished she could turn her emotions off the way one did a light switch, but that simply wasn't realistic.

Hopefully one week in Jamaica would go a long way toward helping her heal.

After an hour and forty-five minutes of driving, Shayna arrived at the Pearson International Airport. She parked, caught the train to Terminal One and dutifully lined up at the counter. A pleasant young woman greeted her with a warm smile. Shayna handed over the paperwork she'd downloaded from the travel agent, along with her passport.

The airline representative punched in Shayna's information, then promptly raised her eyes to hers. "According to your reservation, you're traveling with a Vince Danbury."

"The plan has changed," Shayna said. "I'm traveling alone."

"Oh." The woman's gaze immediately lowered to Shayna's ringless left hand. The impression of the ring that had once been there was visible.

"Let's just say I'm thanking my lucky stars that I learned the truth about him before we said *I do*," Shayna told the woman.

"I'm sorry," the woman said.

"Don't be. Better now than five years and a couple of kids later."

"This is true." The woman printed off a ticket and handed it to Shayna. "Seat 6F. Gate B27. Boarding begins in an hour and fifteen minutes. You have plenty of time."

Shayna took her time heading to the gate, stopping to get a light breakfast—a banana and a yogurt. She also stopped to buy a murder mystery. She tried to act like a woman going on a happy trip, instead of a person going on her supposed honeymoon alone.

At least on the plane she didn't have to worry about making small talk with a stranger. The seat beside her—the one that should have been for Vince—remained unoccupied.

Shayna closed her eyes and tried to sleep as the plane headed for Jamaica.

An hour after arriving at Sangster International Airport in Montego Bay, the chartered bus taking the passengers to the hotel slowed down, then began turning left. Shayna's eyes widened, her spirits soaring when she saw the exterior of the resort.

The Gran Bahia Principe in Runaway Bay, Jamaica, could not have been more beautiful. The grounds were lush with palm trees, well-manicured lawns, and neatly trimmed bushes. An array of colorful flowers added to the hotel's beauty. She broke out in an ear-to-ear grin when she caught a glimpse of the turquoise-blue sea in the distance. This was her first time in the Caribbean, and so far, the landscape was everything she'd dreamed of.

So was the hotel. To put it simply, it was gorgeous. The large columns at the front made it look like a Roman structure—grand and elegant.

Shayna had been sitting alone at the back of the bus, not wanting to engage in small talk, and she waited until everyone had filed off before getting up to exit. The digital clock at the front of the bus read 3:32 p.m.

Outside, the sun was shining in a perfect blue sky. Perhaps the first thing Shayna would do was head to her room, get changed and then find a restaurant where she could have a late lunch. After that, she'd find a spot under a palm tree and continue reading the novel she'd started on the plane.

Shayna got off the bus and stood to the side, knowing it would take a few more minutes for all of the luggage to be unloaded. On the right side of the wide lobby, near the front desk, a woman in a black skirt and white blouse was offering welcome cocktails to the newcomers. Shayna would be sure to get one as soon as she retrieved her luggage.

After a few minutes, she turned back toward the bus and joined the people searching for their suitcases. Hers was navy blue and she would recognize it anywhere, even among a mountain of navy blue suitcases. She wasn't like people who mistakenly took another person's luggage because they all looked so similar.

But she didn't see her suitcase anywhere. It had been with her when she'd gotten off the plane. She'd taken it to the bus. It had to be somewhere.

She approached the bus driver. "My suitcase," she began. "I don't see it anywhere."

"No worries, lovely lady." The man's eyes roamed over her face appreciatively. "The suitcases are being taken into the main lobby." He gestured up the few steps to the left side of the large open foyer.

"Oh. I see." How had she missed that?

"You're beautiful," he told her, letting his eyes roam a little lower. "You here by yourself?"

"Um, no. I'm meeting friends." She handed the man a couple dollars in tip. "Thank you."

Before he could say anything else, she turned and climbed the few steps into the lobby.

The smiling woman with the tray of cocktails approached her, and Shayna took one. The nonalcoholic beverage tasted like a mix of papaya and pineapple. It was refreshing, especially in the island heat, which was a heck of a lot warmer than the weather she'd left in Buffalo.

As Shayna took another sip, she spotted her suitcase, but

before she could retrieve it, she was assured by a bellman that he would watch all the luggage until people had checked in. Then someone would help her get her luggage to the room.

"It's only one piece," Shayna said. "I'll be fine with it on my own."

When she retracted the handle, the man said, "You can leave it with me until you're checked in. Is all right?"

Slowly, she nodded, though she didn't fully meet the man's eyes. She saw that he, too, was checking her out. Maybe he figured her for a tourist who had come to the island to get lucky.

He was cute, but she wasn't interested—even if she did like the sound of his Jamaican accent.

Shayna went to the line at the front desk and waited for her turn to check in. As she did, her eyes roamed. There was a huge stone structure in the middle of the lobby, surrounded by a fountain and foliage. The structure sort of resembled a giant teardrop. Sort of. The floors were a cream-colored marble. The place was elegantly decorated, no doubt about it. The perfect place to spend a honeymoon.

Or a solitary vacation.

Pushing the thought aside, Shayna turned, seeing for the first time that there was a massive terrace on the far left side of the lobby. Happy people sat at tables outside, drinking and enjoying the view. Perhaps that would be a good place to get a bite to eat and read her novel, with the beach and Caribbean Sea as the idyllic backdrop.

Hearing a sudden burst of laughter, she turned and saw a group of people entering the lobby from a hallway near the front steps. It was an extended family by the looks of it, with at least a few women, two men and handful of kids. They were nicely dressed, as though they were heading to an early dinner. One of the men was holding a young girl who had fallen asleep.

Shayna had told her sister that if she never saw another man it would be too soon, but the one carrying the girl was quite something to look at. In fact, she couldn't tear her eyes from him as he strolled across the lobby. He was tall, a little over six feet, with wide shoulders and muscular biceps. Shayna loved football, and this guy had the build of a wide receiver.

The man must have sensed Shayna was staring, because his gaze suddenly turned from his happy family and found hers. His brown eyes sent a jolt of electricity right through her.

Shayna immediately glanced away, uncomfortable. Her heart was beating a little bit faster and she couldn't help wondering why. Guilt that she'd been caught staring?

Or something else?

The man was certainly attractive. He had skin the color of milk chocolate; a strong, chiseled jaw and a seriously nice body evident even beneath the loose white shirt that hung over his black pants. But he was carrying his daughter and was obviously married.

After a few seconds, knowing the man and his family must have passed her by now, she turned to steal another glimpse of him.

Ooh, Lord. What a behind. And those muscular thighs… He was just as attractive from behind.

The man angled his head over his shoulder in her direction, almost as if he sensed her staring again. Her face flaming, Shayna quickly turned her attention back toward the front desk, embarrassed that he would think she'd been checking him out.

But she *had* been checking him out. The realization startled her.

How long had it been since she'd fled the altar? Barely over twenty-four hours. Shayna didn't think she'd be checking anyone out for many months, maybe even years.

As her pulse returned to normal, she cut herself some slack.

As the saying went, she wasn't dead. It wasn't a crime to check out a sexy brother, even if she didn't plan to date ever again.

And there was one reason she'd allowed herself to shamelessly ogle the sexy stranger.

He was safe territory. He was married.

Ten minutes later, Shayna was checked in and had her room key and room number, which the woman at the front desk had told her a bellman would help her find. The same bellman she'd spoken to earlier smiled warmly when she approached him again.

"What room, lovely lady?"

"18326," Shayna said, frowning. The building certainly wasn't eighteen stories high. "You can just direct me, and I'll be fine."

"No worries, mon. I'll take you."

Shayna decided not to argue. There was no point coming across as uptight when the man was only offering help.

The walk to the room went on and on. Every time she thought they were reaching the end, they simply rounded a corner and another corridor came into view. Shayna passed rooms that began with fourteen, fifteen, sixteen—and wondered if they'd reach her room before sunset. The walk seemed to take hours.

But finally, the bellman slowed when he got to the end of what turned out to be the absolute last hallway. "It's a long walk," he explained. "But you have the best view."

The man opened the door for her, inserted the electronic key into a slot on the wall, and flicked on the lights. "When you're in this room, you need to keep this key in the slot to get the lights and air-conditioning working."

The room was warm, but the balcony door was open, sending in some fresh air. It smelled of the sea and also a slightly spicy scent that Shayna figured came from the flowers.

"If the balcony door is open, the air-conditioning shuts off immediately," the man continued.

The room was beautiful. In the middle was a four-poster king-size bed. A dresser was on the opposite wall, beside which was a minifridge. There was a sofa near the balcony window. Across from the sofa was a small round table—upon which was a carafe with a bottle of champagne.

Shayna's heart fluttered. Honeymoon. Of course.

"You also have the best balcony. It's on the corner, so it's much larger than the rooms beside you. They usually give this room to honeymooners."

Shayna's pulse began to race. This was the room where she and Vince were supposed to spend the next seven days and nights in wedded bliss.

Instead…

She stopped the thought before it could finish and reached into her purse. She pulled a few bills out of her wallet and passed them to the man. "Thanks for your help."

He caught her hand as he accepted the money. Caught and held it. Shayna looked at him in surprise.

"You really are a lovely lady," he said softly. "Where's your husband?"

Shayna pulled her hand free, thinking suddenly of her family's concern about her going on this trip alone. She hoped this man wasn't going to be a problem.

"Thanks again for your help," she said in a firm tone, the kind that said she wasn't interested in any more small talk.

The man nodded and headed to the door. "Have a good vacation, pretty lady."

Before he left, Shayna made note of his name. His tag read "Garth." She would file the information away, but she hoped he knew she wasn't interested. If he showed up at her door unannounced, she would be able to tell the front desk who he was.

Shayna closed and locked the door, then slowly strolled through the room. She made her way onto the balcony, which was, as Garth had said, huge. There was a round plastic table in its center, with two plastic chairs. It would be a nice place to eat breakfast in the morning.

The woman at the front desk had explained that Shayna's room was three stories high, even though the third level was directly accessible from the lobby level. Here, the room was at a nice height to see everything around her. Moving forward to the railing, she looked out at the incredible view below. Garth had been right. The walk had been long but worth it. Shayna had never seen water so many shades of blue. To the left there was a large bay populated with sunseekers along the beach and in the water. A number of people were a good fifty yards into the sea, and yet the water only reached to their waists. Clearly, that was a very shallow beach.

Directly below her was a green building. A restaurant, perhaps? Beside that was another building beside a marina where people in bathing suits were eating at plastic tables. That had to be one of the resort's casual eateries.

Shayna's gaze wandered to the right. There she saw a rocky inlet with a smaller beach, at the end of which was a gazebo. No doubt it was a spot where the resort's weddings were held.

In fact, there were people down there now. Some children, some adults.

Wait a minute, Shayna thought, her gaze narrowing. The next instant, she felt a jolt of shock.

The sexy stranger. He was in the gazebo along with his family.

No wonder they'd been nicely dressed. They'd been heading to the gazebo for a wedding.

And when the man turned, Shayna felt another jolt. Out of all the rooms in the hotel, had his gaze landed on *her?*

She quickly hurried into her room, away from the man's gaze. And then she felt stupid.

What was she going to do—run every time she saw him? Stay in her hotel room the entire week to avoid crossing his path?

"It's not like you're about to try and steal another woman's husband," she said to herself. "It's okay to look."

And maybe that's exactly what she needed on this trip. Some eye candy to help soothe the memory of what Vince had done to her.

An attractive man she could admire from afar without any fear that it would lead somewhere.

After all, he was married. Therefore unavailable.

It was perfect.

Chapter 4

The next morning, the sun rose to a glorious day. Shayna stretched, climbed out of bed and immediately went to the balcony window. Pushing the curtains aside, she stared outside and sighed happily, knowing she would never tire of the view.

The previous evening, she'd found the dining hall, enjoyed a solitary dinner that seemed more Mexican than Jamaican, then retired to her room where she'd continued reading after calling home to assure everyone she was okay. Yes, she'd hidden from the world, but she hadn't felt up to small chat with anyone. And she'd had a pleasant time by herself. It was hard to have a bad time when you sat on your balcony and stared out at nature's stunning beauty.

She opened the glass door and stepped onto the balcony. Everything about the resort was magnificent. The beautiful greenery lining the stone paths. The towering palm trees and the low ones. The hibiscus flowers growing in the shrubs. The amazing contrast of light and dark blues in the ocean. The lulling sound of the ocean as it crashed against the shore. And she loved the slightly spicy scent of exotic flowers in the air, something she certainly didn't smell back home in Buffalo.

Shayna smiled. Yes, this was a new day. And she was in paradise. She was going to enjoy it.

Heading back inside, she checked the time on her cell phone. It was after seven in the morning in Jamaica, which meant it was an hour later at home since Jamaica didn't subscribe to daylight saving time. Surprisingly, there wasn't a clock in the room. Maybe the hotel staff had figured that honeymooners would be too wrapped up in each other to care about checking the time of day.

She hadn't eaten much of a dinner last night, and her stomach now grumbled in protest. It was time to head downstairs for breakfast. She got into the shower first, lathering up with the scented body gel the hotel provided, thinking that it was nice not to have to worry about sharing the bathroom with another person. To make her own schedule.

She was determined to look on the bright side.

Once out of the shower, she put her bathing suit on—then a dress to cover it—and packed a beach bag with two hardcover suspense novels. She would lounge by the pool and decide which world to escape into next.

Even though the walk from the front desk had been enormously long, the walk to the restaurant was much shorter. That's because she didn't need to backtrack through the hotel to get to the restaurant. It was directly opposite her building on the other side of the pool.

Shayna enjoyed a leisurely stroll from her building along the path that led to a bridge that crossed over the pool. It was early, but the sun was bright and hot. To her far right, under the terrace outside of the lobby, she saw the word *SPA*. She would definitely take a trip there later, pamper herself.

Shayna climbed the steps to the restaurant and opened the

heavy door. The next moment, her heart caught in her throat. Because the sexy stranger who'd caught her staring at him yesterday was walking directly toward her.

Once again, he was accompanied by three females, two other men this time and the same children from the day before. The little girl the sexy stranger had held yesterday was now wide-awake, jumping with excitement as they exited the restaurant, probably ready to head to the pool or the beach.

Shayna smiled politely at the man and his family, then promptly looked away. She didn't want his wife thinking she was the type of person who would do more than appreciate the good looks of another woman's husband.

And she didn't dare glance over her shoulder, fearing she would give both the man and his wife the wrong impression that she was a flirt.

At home, Shayna would have had a cup of coffee and perhaps a slice of toast for breakfast. But here at this all inclusive resort, she had a freshly made omelet with cheese and vegetables, toast, slices of various fruits *and* a just-baked pastry. She ate and read at the table by herself until her stomach felt like it couldn't hold another crumb.

The food was delicious. If she kept eating at this pace, she'd go home with another twenty pounds on her thighs.

She left the restaurant, appreciating the fact that the resort was as large as it was. All the walking would help burn off the extra calories she would no doubt consume.

As she stepped outside, she scanned the nearby pool area. It was beautiful. It would be a nice place to lounge for a while and read her thriller, let the food digest. Then she would get some exercise by doing several laps in the water.

Even though it was early, there was only one lounge chair left in the shade, at the side of the pool closest to the spa. Shayna could see the beige of the chair's thin mattress, with no towel slung over it to indicate that it was taken. Positioned under a man-made tree created to look like a coconut husk, it was a prime seat. The mattress atop the chair's wooden frame would certainly be more comfortable than the chairs on the opposite side of the pool, which were made of plastic and blue fabric.

The exit of the restaurant was near the towel hut, so first Shayna got herself a towel, then walked briskly to the vacant chair in the shade. Only when she got close to the seat did her legs falter. Sitting two chairs over from the one she planned to claim was the very handsome stranger she apparently would never be able to avoid.

"Brother," she muttered under her breath, then told herself to keep walking toward the chair. What did it matter who was sitting there? The man was married and she could bump into him every other minute for the rest of her stay—it wouldn't matter.

She continued on, her dark sunglasses allowing her to avoid making eye contact with the sexy—and married—stranger. He noticed her—and stared openly at her. Shayna pretended not to notice as she went to the empty lounge chair and settled into it.

Feeling the man's gaze on her, she flitted her eyes to the left without moving her head. She was right. He *was* staring.

Shayna couldn't help scowling, her view on men going down another notch. On Friday night it had plummeted after seeing Vince touching and kissing and then disrobing that stripper. And now, feeling the heat of this man's gaze, she was further disappointed by the male species.

Why on earth was this man giving her more than a casual glance when he was here on this beautiful island with his wife and kids?

It didn't matter. It took two to tango, and Shayna was certainly not going to tango with him.

Nor anyone else.

She put the folded towel behind her head to act as a pillow. Then she dug into her bag and pulled out her serial killer novel. Moments later, she found the page where she'd left off and resumed reading the book. In the story, another young woman's body had just been discovered with a slashed throat and several knife wounds. There wasn't a hint of a love story in sight.

Exactly what Shayna needed.

But even with the gore on the pages to occupy her mind, she was all too aware of the sexy stranger a couple of lounge chairs away. For some reason, her eyes kept surreptitiously flitting in his direction. He and the two other men were talking and laughing. Red Stripe beer bottles were on the table between their chairs.

She noticed all the details. That of the three men, the one she'd first seen had the best body. His shoulders were muscular, his pecs clearly defined. He looked to be related to the man on his right. That man was older, and he had a ring of extra weight around his waist. But he was still attractive, if not as sexy as his brother or cousin—or whoever the undeniably sexy man was.

The man's gaze wandered in her direction, and Shayna quickly held her book higher, making it seem as though her nose had been buried in her story the entire time.

She turned her gaze toward the sprawling pool. Why on earth was this man commanding so much of her attention? For goodness' sake, he was married.

Of course I'm checking him out, Shayna told herself a moment later. She did nothing if not people watch. Her role as a novelist demanded it. She was constantly checking out people, watching their faces as they spoke, their body language as they interacted. Storing every detail in her brain for future use.

She was simply cataloging the details of the man's incredible body for a description in an upcoming story.

Of course that was why she was so intrigued by him. The realization made her sigh with relief.

She went back to her story and continued reading the descriptively brutal passage of the body at the crime scene. And when she heard the scream, she almost thought it came from her imagination.

But when the second frail scream sounded, this time crying out "Daddy!" Shayna jerked her eyes up from the pages of the book. In the pool before her, near a small round island that boasted grass and a palm tree, she saw the little girl struggling to stay afloat.

Shayna bolted into action. The pool was fashioned after a beach, where you walked right in from the shallow shore. Shayna sprinted right into the water, dress and all, moving as fast as she could to get to the little girl. She was aware of the commotion around her, but she blocked it out. Blocked it out until she reached the little girl and pulled her into the safety of her arms.

No sooner than she had the crying child, someone was reaching for the girl. Shayna quickly looked to her left. The sexy man and the two other men were there, but it was the brother or cousin who was taking the little girl from Shayna's arms.

"Daddy!" The girl coughed. "Daddy!"

The man enveloped the little girl in an embrace. It was the same little girl who'd been so eager to get to the pool when Shayna had been heading in for breakfast. Shayna gazed down at the two older boys and three older girls in the pool, probably between the ages of six and eight. Their small faces were marred with concern.

"How did she get over here, Isaiah?" the man holding the crying young girl demanded.

"I don't know—she just—"

It was the younger of the two boys who'd spoken, and he looked like he was going to cry.

"It's all right." The voice was just as sexy as the man. Shayna tried her best not to look at him. "You called for our help. That was smart. Very smart."

Isaiah nodded bravely, and the sexy man clamped his hand down on his shoulder in a gesture of support.

And that's when Shayna realized she shouldn't still be standing there. That she was observing—intruding   when she should have moved back already.

She turned and started walking away. She didn't get more than two steps before she felt a hand on her arm.

"Hey," came the deep voice. Shayna turned, her heart thundering as she did. Piercing brown eyes met and held her gaze. "Thank you."

"You don't have to thank me. I did what anyone else would do."

"No, thank you," the man insisted. "My niece was drowning—and we can't thank you enough for your quick action."

His *niece?*

"Yes, thank you." The man holding the little girl spoke now. The young girl, maybe three, was wailing and coughing. More frightened than anything else, Shayna knew.

But thank God she was okay.

"You're welcome," Shayna said. "I'm glad I could help."

Then she headed back to her lounge chair. Her dress was soaking from the chest down, and she pulled it over her head. That's when she noticed *him*. Walking toward her.

The look in his eyes made her stomach flutter, which was completely inappropriate. Even if he wasn't the young girl's father as she'd assumed, he was likely still the father of at least one of the children. Or at the very least, married to one of the three women who were nowhere in sight.

Shayna pretended not to notice him and instead concentrated on laying her dress over the back of the chair to air it out.

"Sorry you got your dress wet," the man said.

"It's perfectly okay," Shayna told him, hoping her voice was as flat as possible. "It'll dry."

The man was near her now, only a couple of feet away. He extended his hand, "I'm Donovan."

Shayna hesitated. She almost didn't say her name. What was the point? But she decided that simply stating her name was not an invitation to begin an affair.

"I'm Shayna."

"Nice name."

Shayna almost rolled her eyes, but she didn't. Instead she glanced around, looking to see where the three women were. She'd assumed they'd gone for a bathroom break or perhaps to the nearby bar.

She saw no one.

"I'm sorry," Donovan said. "Are you expecting someone?"

"No. Just…checking the place out." She paused a beat. "Which children are yours?"

Donovan seemed momentarily confused. Then he said, "Oh. None. But I'm a proud uncle."

"Are you trying?" The question came from Shayna's lips before she could stop it. It was none of her business, of course, but she was trying—as eloquently as possible—to let this man know that she wasn't the least bit interested in someone who was married.

"Trying to have children?" Donovan once again sounded surprised at her question.

"You seem to be a very loving family," she said, gesturing

to the children and other men. "And you're clearly an attentive uncle. I'm sure you must want kids with your *wife*."

Donovan's eyes widened in slight surprise. Then he nodded in understanding. "Aah. Well, I suppose if I had a wife I'd be trying. But I'm single."

Now it was Shayna's turn to look surprised. "You— You're not married?"

He flashed his naked left ring finger. "Nope."

"But I… Who are those women you're with?"

"My sister, my brother's wife and my cousin's wife. Two of the kids are my brother's, three are my sister's and one is my cousin's. Another cousin just got married yesterday. You haven't seen her yet because she and her new husband are… well, they're spending a lot of time indoors. Anything else you want to know?" Donovan added, a warm smile playing on his lips.

"No." Shayna shook her head briskly. "I'm sorry…I had no right to be nosy."

"But you thought I was married."

Shayna glanced away. "To be honest, yes."

"Now you know I'm not."

The way he said the words made Shayna's eyes jerk to his. And when they did, something in his gaze made her pulse race.

Donovan *wanted* her to know he wasn't married. And there could be only one reason for that.

He was interested.

The charge she'd felt as she'd looked at him the night before had come not just from her appreciation of his good looks but also from *his* attraction to her.

"Is this your first time in Jamaica?" he asked.

Lord, but the man was fine. Shayna allowed herself a moment to stare at him without guilt. At his broad shoulders and perfectly sculpted chest.

But that was all she would allow.

She looked away. "Yes. It's my first time here."

"Mine, too," Donovan said. "Beautiful place for a wedding."

"Right." Shayna smiled tightly. The last thing she wanted to think about was how perfect the place was for a wedding.

"So, where are you from?" Donovan asked.

"Why?"

"Excuse me?" Donovan asked.

Sighing softly, Shayna crossed her arms over her chest. She knew where this was going, and she wasn't interested. Yes, the man was gorgeous, but she wasn't on the island for a meaningless fling. She was getting over her broken heart.

"I'm going to come right out and say this," Shayna began. "I think you're a perfectly nice man and all, but I'm not interested in getting to know anyone."

"Ouch."

"I'm sorry," Shayna said, realizing she'd been far too abrupt. "I was really rude, wasn't I? It's just…"

"Just what?" Donovan asked.

"Just…" She paused. Exhaled sharply. "Nothing I feel like talking about right now. So let's just leave things off with my apology. I'm not normally this rude."

"Donovan!"

Both Shayna and Donovan turned following the sound of the voice. Donovan's brother, cousin and the children were back at their lounge chairs, drying their bodies with towels.

The father of Donovan's niece—which meant the man was Donovan's brother—said, "We've got to get going if we're going to make the bus."

Despite herself, Shayna asked, "You're going on an excursion?"

"Yeah. We're doing the dolphin 'touch' experience. Meaning we don't get to swim with the dolphins, but we can go in the water with them and pet them. It better be good. It's costing an arm and a leg."

"What about the women?"

"It's just the guys and kids. The ladies said they needed a break from being moms, so they're doing a spa day."

"Donovan!"

"Relax, Antwon. I'm coming."

"The bus leaves at nine."

"I know, I know." Donovan waved off his brother's concern, then turned back to Shayna. "It was nice to meet you, Shayna. Sorry that you're having a rough time, but I do hope that you have a lovely day."

Shayna felt like dirt. Here Donovan was, trying to be nice, and she had taken out her frustration with men—Vince in particular—on him. What was the harm in making small talk? Small talk did not equal reciprocation of affection.

She wanted to apologize again, but instead she simply said, "Thanks. You have a good day, too."

Donovan smiled again—and Lord if it wasn't the most charismatic smile in the world—then turned and headed back to his family. Shayna sat back down and picked her book up. But she didn't even glance at the pages. Instead, she turned and watched as Donovan dried that magnificent body of his with the large blue towel.

And when he slung the towel over his shoulder and looked her way, Shayna didn't turn her head. Instead, she raised her hand and gave a little wave.

It was the least she could do to show she regretted her ungracious behavior.

Chapter 5

"You like her," Antwon said, clamping a hand down on Donovan's shoulder as they stood at the front of the hotel, waiting to get on the bus that would take them to Ocho Rios.

Donovan faced his brother, not having heard what he'd said. "Hmm?"

"I've been talking to you for five minutes, and I bet you didn't hear a word I said. You've been staring off into the distance. You're thinking about that woman from the pool, aren't you?"

Donovan's eyebrows shot up at the statement. How had his brother read his thoughts?

Antwon chuckled. "Think I don't know my little brother? You like her."

"She's cute," Donovan admitted.

"She's *hot*," Antwon corrected.

Donovan shrugged, playing nonchalant.

"Are you gonna pretend you didn't notice?"

"No, she's definitely hot." Donovan had thought of nothing else since they'd left the pool to go back to the room. Shayna was gorgeous. He'd noticed her immediately the day before. He'd also noticed that she was alone. For him, that had been good. But her comment to him earlier made it clear she didn't want to be bothered.

"Why do I sense a *but?*" Antwon asked.

"I tried to make conversation, but she wasn't interested," Donovan stated flatly.

"So you try again."

Ennis, their cousin, had been tending to the children in front of them, but hearing the conversation, took a step toward them and spoke. "He's been out of the game so long, Antwon, he doesn't remember how to play."

"Hey," Donovan said, frowning. "I still got game. But if someone's not interested—"

"She's interested," Ennis said, confident she was.

That perked Donovan up. "Why do you say that?"

"Because every time your back was turned, she was checking you out."

"Really?" Donovan asked. Shayna's rejection had left him feeling out of sorts, but with his cousin's comment, he was now feeling better.

"Really." This from Antwon. "I saw it. Then you'd turn her way, and she'd quickly put her head back in her book."

Donovan placed his hands on his hips, a smile playing on the edges of his mouth. "Really?"

"Oh, yeah," Ennis said.

"Wow. I'm surprised. She totally blew me off when I talked to her."

Antwon slung an arm across Donovan's shoulders. "That's exactly how Lynda was when I first met her. Gave me the cold shoulder most of the time. Did she mean it? No. She wanted me to chase her. Show her I was really interested. Women love that."

You'd never know it now. Lynda and Antwon were as lovey-dovey as two people could be. It was nice to see.

And it was exactly what Donovan wanted for himself. In fact, two and half years ago he'd had all reason to expect that he would be enjoying that kind of marriage right now—but things had gone tragically wrong.

"You should have invited her to come along," Ennis said.

"Right." Donovan rolled his eyes. "Like she'd want to be the only woman on our trip. She doesn't know us."

"That's gonna change," Ennis said and smirked.

"Enough about Shayna already," Donovan said, but inside he was smirking, too.

"Shayna," Antwon said, his voice teasing. "Nice name."

Donovan punched his brother's arm. "Seriously. Enough."

But the truth was, he didn't mind the friendly teasing. It had been years since his brother or cousin could bug him about any woman.

Keira, Ennis's five-year-old daughter, tugged on his shirt. "Daddy, Tamara won't share her drink."

"Okay, sweetheart," Ennis said and stepped forward to deal with the children.

"Good, there's the bus," Donovan said, seeing the large tour bus pull up in front of the hotel. "Let's get this show on the road."

The bus came to a stop in front of them, and the children, who'd been antsy, dutifully lined up.

"Hey," Antwon said, putting a hand on Donovan's shoulder.

Donovan faced him. "Hmm?"

"Seriously, it's nice to see you interested in someone again."

Had he been that obvious? All Donovan had done was talk to Shayna. And he hadn't gotten to say that much.

"I know you've had a rough time since Nina died," his brother went on. "But I think she'd approve."

At the mention of Nina, Donovan felt a spasm of sadness in his gut. He supposed he always would when he thought of the fiancée he had loved.

And lost.

Two and a half years ago, he'd been on track to marry the woman of his dreams. And then they'd gotten the devastating news that she had breast cancer. It had been caught too late. The cancer had spread to her lymph nodes and bones. Six months later, she was gone.

And so were his dreams of forever.

"Sorry," Antwon said. "I didn't mean to bring you down. I'm just saying, it'll be good for you to start dating."

"Yeah," Donovan said softly. "I know."

The thought of dating had been too painful in the beginning. And even after a year had passed, he hadn't gotten Nina out of his heart. He hadn't been against meeting someone new, someone as special as Nina was. It was just that no one had sparked his interest.

Until now.

For some reason, though he'd just met her, he felt a really strong attraction to her. And yes, she was beautiful, but it was more than that.

Donovan didn't know where things might lead with Shayna, if they led anywhere at all. But after two long years as a single man, the part of him he thought had died along with Nina had suddenly come back to life.

Long after he'd left to go on his excursion, Shayna couldn't get Donovan off her mind. She sat on her lounge chair, hardly retaining what she read because she couldn't stop thinking about the man.

She still felt bad for being so gruff with him. Honestly, there was no excuse for that. Clearly, her emotions were frayed after the stressful ordeal with Vince. She would have to make a concerted effort not to take her frustration out on anyone else.

But there was another reason why she kept thinking about Donovan. One she didn't really want to admit to herself.

So she began to read her novel again, but about a minute later, she realized that her eyes were merely passing over the words without truly following the story. Her heart fluttering a little, Shayna lowered the book and let her mind go where it wanted to.

Back to Donovan.

It wasn't just that she felt bad about how she'd spoken to him. If she was honest with herself, she couldn't get him off her mind because of the shocking knowledge that he was single.

When she'd assumed he was married, she'd considered him safe. She could watch him from afar, appreciate his utterly sexy body and not have to worry about a flirtation developing.

But now…

Now, not only was Donovan unmarried but he seemed interested in getting to know her.

Shayna rolled her eyes at the thought. Who was she fooling? He *might* have been interested—but surely she'd turned him off with her attitude.

Which was just as well.

Because she couldn't deny that there was something about the man, something that intrigued her. Far more than it should for a woman who should, right now, be Mrs. Vince Danbury.

Vince… Shayna snorted in derision at the mere thought of him. It was amazing how, with his betrayal, she no longer saw him as attractive. And even on his best day, he didn't compare to Donovan.

An image of Donovan came into Shayna's mind again, and to her surprise she felt a little tingle in her stomach. He'd looked so incredibly breathtaking when he'd walked toward her after coming from the pool. Beads of water had glistened on his smooth, dark chest. With only swimming trunks on, she'd gotten an unrestricted view of his well-defined abs, wide shoulders, and brawny arms. The man had zero body fat and muscles in all the right places. Which included those strong thighs of his.

He honestly looked as though he could have been cast from a mold for the perfect man.

He was the kind of man who drew women's eyes from across the room, which was no doubt why she'd been drawn to him last night. He was movie-star handsome with a winning smile that would melt any woman's heart.

Shayna liked to think that you could tell a lot about a man by his smile. And in Donovan's bright and earnest smile she saw someone who was honest and down-to-earth. Unlike men with less looks who were overly cocky, Donovan seemed real—not like the type to think that because he was gorgeous and had a great body that made him more special than any other man.

He'd been genuinely nice—and Shayna hadn't expected that. Not after she'd figured him a married man with a wandering eye.

She had fully believed him not only married but a father. Which was why she'd had such a negative reaction to the idea that he was checking her out at all. And why she'd been as snippy as she had when he'd started talking to her.

She'd wrongly seen him as another Vince.

"Why am I still thinking about him?" Shayna asked herself. She was on page eighty-seven of her novel—and she'd reread the same paragraph at least six times. With another murder in this riveting book, she was anxious to see how the story would play out. And yet, she couldn't concentrate on anything she was reading.

Shayna closed the book and eased her body up. Her gaze traveled over the pool area. There were a good number of people here, but Shayna supposed there would be a lot more if this were February or March, when the winter blues back home had kicked in with full force. There were kids, parents, couples. Babies in the kiddie pool, happily stomping around in the water. Old people lying on their backs, taking in as much sun as possible. Young couples holding hands as they lay on chairs that were side by side. People of different races. Everyone either playing or relaxing.

Everyone except her.

Of all the people here, Shayna would bet that she was the only one in this idyllic place with a heavy heart.

Maybe it was Donovan talking about his cousin who'd just gotten married or watching the couples young and old that seemed to be very much in love. But Shayna suddenly felt very alone.

It was impossible to forget that she was a woman who was *supposed* to be on her honeymoon.

She didn't miss Vince—not in the least—but she did feel… uncomfortable. Like she had a tattoo on her forehead that said she was a woman who'd just been jilted.

Maybe she should have taken her sister up on her offer to come here with her. With her sister along, she could go on excursions. Do the fun touristy things that other people at this resort were doing with their friends and families.

What's your problem? she asked herself. *You're having one difficult moment and you're already wishing you weren't here by yourself? You knew this week wasn't going to be a vacation. It was supposed to be time for rest, relaxation and reflection.*

She may have resolved to put Vince firmly behind her, but she wasn't dumb enough to believe that the memory of his betrayal wasn't going to hurt. The whole reason for being in Jamaica—other than the fact that the trip had been paid for—was to be in a pretty place with lots of sunshine while she went through the stages required to truly move on.

Shayna put her book back in her tote bag and got up. Her dress was still mostly wet, so she first draped the towel over her arm and put the dress on top of that. It was time for a walk around the extensive property. A walk for exercise and to clear her mind.

But before going on her stroll, Shayna wanted a drink. She made her way to the bar and ordered herself a piña colada with dark rum. Her eyes drank in the sights near her while the bartender prepared her drink. The bar boasted a swim-up pool bar on one side, where you didn't even have to exit the water to get your drink of choice. In that part of the winding pool, people were doing water aerobics to a lively reggae beat. She watched them jogging on the spot.

"Why don't you join us?" a man asked. He was dark-skinned, spoke with a Jamaican accent and had both the smile and body of Taye Diggs. Even though he was looking at her, Shayna glanced over her shoulder.

No one was there.

"Yes, I'm talking to you," the man said, his smile never fading even as he continued to jog.

Shayna realized he must be the instructor. "No, thanks. I'm heading for a walk."

The man's eyes lingered on her face before lazily traveling down her body.

Shayna's eyes widened in surprise. Another man brazenly

checking her out. Back at home, she got her share of attention—but nothing like this. Here, men didn't hide their appreciation for a beautiful woman.

If she were a different person, she would lap up the attention. Or perhaps if she were here with her sister or some girlfriends, she'd end up flirting in a carefree and fun way.

But she was a woman on her solo honeymoon, one who wanted to put men out of her mind for the week.

That's what she told herself. But even as she started off to explore a part of the hotel grounds she hadn't yet seen, she found herself remembering the way Donovan had smiled at her—particularly when he'd realized that she'd thought he was married.

It was charming, she realized. Yes, Donovan had a certain charm and natural charisma. Add to those qualities a nice personality and amazing physique and you had yourself the perfect man.

Exactly the kind of man Shayna would write about in one of her books.

And she suddenly understood why Donovan was so appealing to her.

When her friends had teased her about not finding love in her real life and she countered that she would never settle, it had always been a man like Donovan she had imagined in her life. A man with a great smile, natural charm and a killer body. But she'd never truly expected to find the total package—at least not as perfect as it had been in her fantasies. Vince had come close with his combination of charm and good looks, even if he didn't have six-pack abs. But she could honestly say, at least by appearance and first impressions, that Donovan was a ten. At least a ten on her meter of all-around attractiveness.

So that's what it was. He was gorgeous, with a stunning

smile—the kind of guy who would suit her well in her fantasies. That's why she couldn't stop thinking about him.

And in the wake of her heartbreak, maybe she *needed* that kind of eye candy. A delicious distraction from her real world.

Oh, she knew what her friend Christine would say. After losing her husband to another woman, Christine would tell her to go for it with Donovan. That enjoying herself with Donovan would go a long way to help her get over Vince. Christine had had a casual affair after her husband's betrayal, and it had done wonders for her self-esteem. Even if only temporarily.

Shayna stopped abruptly, taking a sip of her drink to cool her down. How on earth had her thoughts gone from thinking Donovan was attractive to imagining that she might have a fling with him?

I'll blame it on the rum, she told herself, finishing off her piña colada.

But she was all too aware that the rum had nothing to do with it.

Chapter 6

After her walk, Shayna went back to the room. The heat and the alcohol had made her a little tired, so she opted for a nap.

She dreamed about Donovan.

When she woke up and realized that she hadn't escaped the man even in her sleep, she knew that she was having some sort of emotional breakdown. It simply wasn't like her to think about a man she didn't know to this degree. What she needed to do was put Donovan out of her mind and get on with the task of gaining perspective on her relationship with Vince.

But after half an hour of sitting on her balcony and contemplating why she'd chosen the wrong man, she found herself bored by the topic. Honestly, there was nothing to learn. And Shayna wasn't the type of woman who blamed herself for a man's issues. The fact was that Vince was a cheater. She'd been a good woman who had fallen for the wrong man. Simple as that. She hated when people—women especially—accepted blame for behavior that wasn't theirs.

That wasn't to say she didn't care. She did. A part of her didn't know if she would ever be able to trust her heart to another man. But surprisingly, she wasn't grieving in the way she thought she might.

And she had a sneaking feeling it was because she had another man to occupy her thoughts.

Putting down her novel, Shayna stood and walked to the balcony's railing, where she looked out at the sea. She was in paradise and enjoying it—and she wasn't going to beat herself up for her thoughts.

It didn't really matter how she got over Vince, as long as she did. If flirting with Donovan helped her in that goal…

Whoa. *Flirting?*

Shayna chuckled. Well, she was certainly getting ahead of herself. After how she'd spoken to Donovan earlier, did she really expect him to talk to her again, much less flirt with her?

Shayna went back to reading, finishing one novel and starting another one. Shortly before six, she decided to go downstairs for dinner. But instead of going casually, without any makeup as she had the previous evening, she put on mascara and lipstick. And she fussed over her hair, instead of drawing it back into a ponytail. Satisfied that it fell nicely around her face, she found her red sundress and put it on. It was the same one her sister had; they'd bought them when they'd gone shopping together.

It was Shayna's favorite dress. The color was bold and sexy and complemented her caramel-toned skin.

She was all too aware that she had made herself look good in the hopes of seeing Donovan.

But it wasn't that she was out to seduce him. She just wanted to look respectable when she apologized to him again. She felt a second apology was in order, given her out-of-character behavior. Hopefully he would see that she was a decent person, and perhaps she might end up with a friend to hang out with for the rest of the week.

But Shayna didn't see Donovan in the dining hall.

And instead of sitting at a table, she found herself wandering back out of the restaurant. She remembered what the woman at the front desk had told her at check-in—that there were various à la carte restaurants at the resort, like Japanese and Italian, but that you had to make reservations to eat there.

Shayna strolled along the path outside the main dining hall in the direction of the front of the hotel. Soon, she found a set of stairs and took them up. She ended up on the terrace, which was much larger than she'd originally thought. It was a lot wider than the adjoining lobby.

Strolling to the edge of the terrace, she stared down at the pool. The sun was beginning to set, and lights beneath the water had turned on. In the distance, waves crashed against the shoreline. Palm trees swayed gently in the breeze.

Shayna was struck again by just how beautiful this place was. It really was the kind of place you wanted to share with someone.

"Hello, there."

Shayna spun around at the sound of the voice, her heart beating. But the face she saw was not the one she expected.

It was Garth.

"Oh," she said. "Hello."

"It's a beautiful view, isn't it?"

"Yes," Shayna agreed.

"But not as beautiful as you."

Inwardly, Shayna cringed. She didn't need this. Didn't want this. "I was just heading down to have dinner."

"I can walk with you."

Shayna looked over her shoulder into the lobby as she headed toward the stairs she had just ascended. She didn't see Donovan nor any members of his family.

So she started down the stairs, and Garth fell into step beside her. Instinct told her he was going to be a pest, and she wished he would go away.

"Tell me something," he said.

"What?" Shayna asked, facing him.

"How come a beautiful woman like you is here on this island by herself?"

"People don't travel here alone?"

"Not typically, no."

Hitting the main level, Shayna walked briskly as she talked. "I wanted a nice vacation. No one could come with me, so I went by myself."

She caught Garth's gaze, saw the skeptical expression on his face. "Really?"

"Yes, really," she told him.

"Because you had a bottle of champagne in your room," Garth went on. "We put that in rooms for honeymooners."

Garth paused, and Shayna knew he was fishing, but she didn't feel like talking to him about her failed wedding. It was none of his business.

Garth continued. "What happened? Did you cancel your wedding or just postpone it?"

Thankfully, they were at the restaurant's doors. Forcing a smile, Shayna faced Garth. "Thank you for your concern," she said amicably, "but it's not something I feel like talking about."

Garth was still wearing his bellman outfit, so Shayna knew he wouldn't follow her inside. Before he could say anything else, she made her way into the restaurant.

Fear had her heart beating a little bit faster. She was starting to get the feeling that Garth might become a bit of a problem.

She hoped he was just chatty and trying to be nice to the

hotel guests. Or that if he *was* interested, he wouldn't cross any lines.

"Table for two?" the hostess asked her.

"No, one." Shayna smiled brightly, leaving no opportunity for the hostess to possibly feel sorry for her.

She led her to a small table at the back of the restaurant. No sooner than she sat, a male waiter approached to take her drink order.

"A piña colada, please."

Shayna placed her novel on the table so people would know it was occupied, then made her way toward the buffet area. But she stopped midstride, her heart pounding harder when she saw who was about twenty feet away from her.

Donovan.

She would know that body anywhere.

His back was toward her as he was filling his plate with salad. He wasn't with any of his family members, but Shayna was sure they must be here somewhere, likely at a table on the other side of the restaurant.

She began to walk again, slowly, wondering why she felt so nervous about speaking to him. All she wanted to do was apologize.

So she picked up her pace. When she was about two feet away from him, he turned toward the selection of breads. He must have caught her in his peripheral vision, because he suddenly whipped his head in her direction.

Seeing her, his eyes lit up. And then there was that smile again.

Gorgeous and charming. He was that and then some.

Shayna returned the smile, then took another step toward him. "Hi."

"Wow." His eyes traveled over her from head to toe. "You look amazing."

A wave of heat washed over her. She'd gotten dolled up

for him, after all. It was nice that he liked how she looked. "Thank you."

Someone brushed against Shayna as he passed her to get to the salad bar. Realizing she was in the way, she moved toward the table with the breads. So did Donovan.

"I just wanted to apologize again for earlier," Shayna said. "I feel awful for being so rude."

"Apology accepted," Donovan told her. "Don't worry about it."

Shayna took a plate and began to peruse the selection of breads beside Donovan. "So, did you have a good time today?"

"It was amazing," he told her. "The kids had a blast and so did the guys."

"Good." Shayna snagged a whole-wheat roll. She noticed that Donovan's plate was full, so it was unlikely that he'd walk the buffet area with her. "Well, I just wanted to make sure I apologized again," she told him. "Enjoy your dinner."

"Where are you sitting?" Donovan asked her.

She pointed in the direction. "Over there."

"Alone?"

"Yes."

"Why don't you join us?"

Her stomach fluttered with nerves. "Oh, I couldn't. I don't want to intrude on your family."

Donovan thought for a moment, considering something. Then he said, "How about I join you?"

Shayna's heart slammed against her rib cage at the suggestion. "You want to join me?"

"Why not?"

"But your family—"

"Will be fine without me."

"Oh." Lord, she was nervous. She *wanted* Donovan to join

her. It would be a welcome change to dining alone. "In that case, sure."

"I'll just tell them where I'll be so they don't wonder."

Shayna nodded, then continued on through the buffet, opting for jerk chicken with rice as well as cucumber salad. By the time she turned to head back to the table, she saw Donovan standing near the perimeter of the buffet area, waiting for her.

He smiled softly as she approached him. Forget a ten out of ten. He was at least a fifteen.

Shayna rounded the corner to her table, wondering if Donovan was checking her out from behind the way she had done with him. Reaching her table, she placed her plate down. The waiter had already brought the piña colada over.

"A book?" Donovan said, seeing the novel. "That was your company this evening?"

Shayna nodded as she sat. "I love reading."

"So do I, but..."

"But what?"

"Well, to be frank, I can't imagine why you're here in such a beautiful place alone."

From Donovan, the comment didn't unnerve her the way it had when Garth had mentioned it.

"Who says I'm alone?" she asked, deciding to have a little fun with him.

"Oh." Donovan looked surprised. "You're not? I just assumed."

"The way I assumed you were married." A beat passed, and Shayna chuckled softly. "I'm kidding. I am here alone."

Donovan's eyes lit up again, and Shayna could swear he was relieved. "Awww...I see. You're trying to trick me."

"Just having a little fun. I'm not always uptight."

"Hey, forget about this morning." Donovan lifted the fork beside his plate. "Bon appétit."

"Bon appétit," Shayna repeated as she spiked a cucumber.

They ate in silence for a few minutes before Donovan spoke. "So," he began, "are you here for a week, or just a few days?"

"A week."

"And will you be alone for the entire time? Or is someone joining you?"

Shayna swallowed her mouthful of food before speaking. "I'm on my own for the entire week."

Donovan nodded. "Does the fact that you're here alone have anything to do with what you mentioned earlier? That you're going through something?"

"Yes," Shayna admitted. "As a matter of fact, it does."

The waiter approached the table at that moment, asking if Donovan wanted anything to drink. "I'd love a rum punch," he told the young man.

When the waiter was out of earshot, Donovan continued speaking. "If you feel like talking about anything, I'm here."

"Thank you." Shayna appreciated the offer and his unobtrusive manner. He didn't automatically ask what was bothering her, leaving the decision to talk about it up to her.

The waiter reappeared, passed Donovan his drink and then disappeared again.

"You asked me where I was from earlier, and I didn't tell you," Shayna said. "I'm from Buffalo, New York."

"The B-lo."

"You've been to Buffalo?" Shayna asked, surprised.

"In college, I had a friend who got drafted by the Buffalo Bills."

"Really?" Shayna asked, perking up.

"You a Bills fan?"

"One of the biggest. What's your friend's name?"

"You wouldn't know him. At least I don't think. His name is Tony Ray, but he didn't make it past the training camp. He tried for two seasons but didn't make the team. So he gave up, took a job with Microsoft and moved to Washington state."

"So you play football?" Shayna asked. That would explain the body. Maybe he still did. She wouldn't be surprised to learn that he played professionally.

"Only with my buddies. In my spare time."

"Well, you look like you could be a football player."

"I did play in college. But only for fun. I never had aspirations to play professionally. It's a tough game on your body."

It was clear that Donovan took care of his body. To keep his muscles so honed, he had to work out regularly.

"Where are you from?" Shayna asked him.

"Laurel, Maryland. Not too far from D.C."

Shayna finished off her drink, then looked around for the waiter. The piña coladas were delicious. She wouldn't mind another.

"You need another drink?" Donovan asked.

"If the waiter comes back around."

Donovan eased his chair back and stood. "I'll find him for you. Another piña colada?"

"Yes, please."

Shayna's eyes traveled over Donovan's body as he walked away from the table. He was dressed in a pair of black dress pants and a short-sleeved black shirt that clung to his muscles. Oh, but the man was fine.

She loved his strong, confident, sexy walk. To look at him, the man was a great catch. Which had her wondering why he wasn't here with someone special.

A few minutes later, he returned with another piña colada. Grinning at her, he placed it on the table before her.

Shayna's stomach fluttered. He was sexy, gorgeous *and* a gentleman. A lethal combination.

Shayna made quick work of drinking the second piña colada, while listening to Donovan talk about how much fun the kids had had with the dolphins earlier and some of the other excursions they had planned for the week. By the time she finished the drink, she had a buzz going.

"Sounds like you're going to have a blast," Shayna said. "I probably won't get off the resort."

"You're welcome to come with us," Donovan said. "We're going to Dunn's River Falls on Wednesday. I'm really looking forward to that."

Dunn's River Falls. Shayna's stomach churned, the food and drink she'd consumed suddenly feeling heavy in her belly. She and Vince had planned to head to the falls. They'd researched Jamaica online before their wedding and learned that Dunn's River Falls was the island's biggest attraction. The thrill of the experience came in climbing the towering waterfall, more than six hundred feet tall, and with its lush, tropical setting, Shayna had imagined how romantic it would be.

"I wouldn't want to intrude," she said, her tone flat.

"You wouldn't be intruding. And since we're going on Wednesday, it'll be easy enough to book the excursion with the front desk tomorrow. If you want."

"I'll think about it," Shayna told Donovan, then placed her utensils on her plate and pushed it forward, leaving one whole piece of the jerk chicken untouched. "Thank you for your company, Donovan." Again, her tone was flat. "It's been pleasant."

Donovan watched as Shayna dabbed at her mouth with her napkin, wondering if she'd just dismissed him. But he wasn't near ready to be done with her yet.

She didn't meet his eyes as she carefully folded her napkin.

In fact, she seemed to be busying herself with her hands as a way to avoid looking at him.

Something about her demeanor had changed when he'd mentioned Dunn's River Falls. He wasn't sure what was going on with her, but he assumed it had to do with a man.

"What are you doing after dinner?" Donovan asked suddenly.

Shayna raised her eyes to his. "Tonight?"

"Yeah," Donovan said. "What are your plans?"

"Other than curling up with my book and relaxing?"

"That's no way to spend a night in Jamaica."

"No?"

"No. Absolutely not." Donovan paused a beat. "Why don't you spend the night with me?"

Chapter 7

Donovan didn't have to see Shayna's eyes widen in surprise to realize how his words had sounded. He'd caught the slip the moment the words had fallen off his tongue.

"I didn't mean that how it sounded," Donovan quickly said, feeling foolish. "I meant—"

He stopped speaking when he saw that Shayna was softly laughing.

"What can I say?" he went on. "I've got foot-in-mouth disease. And you can stop laughing now."

To his surprise, Shayna kept giggling, a hysterical fit of laughter, almost as if she couldn't control herself. Surely she wasn't having that good a laugh at his expense.

"I'm sorry," she finally said. "It's just that if I don't laugh I'll—"

Shayna stopped abruptly, covering her face with a hand. Donovan's eyes narrowed as he regarded her with concern. Was she laughing—or was she crying?

"Excuse me," she said, and abruptly pushed her chair

back and stood. Then she hustled toward the front door of the restaurant.

Donovan stood, staring after her, wondering what on earth had just happened. Then he glanced at the table. Her novel was still there. So was her tote bag. Obviously, she must be planning to return.

But what had happened to her? One minute she'd appeared to be having a lovely time. Then her mood had changed.

He sat back down, and the minutes that passed seemed like hours. He would wait a while longer for her to return, and if she didn't, he would head outside to look for her. Make sure she was okay.

A few minutes later, when she still hadn't returned, Donovan picked up Shayna's tote bag and her novel, then made his way to the restaurant's exit. He was determined to find her.

Because he had a feeling she wasn't all right.

Shayna rushed into the restroom, tears already streaming down her face before she could step into a stall.

What was wrong with her? She'd been having a perfectly pleasant time. Then Donovan had mentioned Dunn's River Falls and she'd begun to lose it. She hadn't been able to control her excessive laughter, then the laughter had turned to tears.

She figured she'd go through at least one emotional meltdown this week, but she hadn't expected it when she was having such a nice dinner with Donovan.

He was supposed to be a distraction from her drama.

And yet, being with him reminded her of the fact that the week was supposed to be playing out entirely differently than it was.

Shayna wadded up some toilet paper and used it to dab at her face and cheeks. It was the mention of Dunn's River Falls that had triggered her emotion. Vince had been excited as he'd shown her the brochures about Jamaica from the travel agent, and she had been particularly excited when they'd checked out the photos of Dunn's River Falls online. How had Vince so easily thrown everything away?

Shayna dabbed at her eyes, then straightened her spine. The hell of it was, she wasn't really crying over Vince. But the thought of another man, who truly was a gentleman, offering to do with her some of the things she and Vince had planned to do…it had reminded her of how quickly her life had gone from one extreme to another. From engaged woman to single and back on the market.

And there was also the undeniable attraction she felt to Donovan. She couldn't wrap her mind around it, especially not given the timing, but neither could she deny it.

And it kind of scared her. Because where would this attraction to Donovan lead?

Would flirting with him help lead to her moving on? Or would it leave her suffering another broken heart at the end of the week? Because Shayna wasn't all that good at casual flirting or casual hookups. Her friend Christine had been able to have a carefree affair after her husband had left her, but another of Shayna's friends, Cheryl, had been devastated when a relationship that had begun on vacation in Hawaii had ended a couple of months later.

"And why are you even thinking about this?" Shayna asked herself. "For God's sake, you've had one dinner with him."

After which, he would certainly think her insane, if her brusque attitude with him in the morning hadn't led him to that conclusion already.

Shayna straightened her spine and exited the stall. Then she went to the mirror and checked out her reflection. Her eyes were a little moist, but hopefully Donovan wouldn't realize she'd been crying.

Her lips could use another coat of lipstick, but of course,

she'd left her tote bag inside. So she simply smoothed her hair then cleaned up the smeared makeup around her eyes. Satisfied that she looked as good as she was going to, she inhaled a deep breath to calm the last of her frayed nerves. Feeling better, she exited the bathroom.

And then she stopped dead in her tracks. Because Donovan was standing there. She couldn't have been more surprised.

"Hey," he said, taking a step toward her.

"Hey," she replied, realizing that her heart was pounding from the mere sight of him. How was this possible? And how had he known where she was? To get to the restrooms, you had to leave the restaurant and enter the doors along the side wall of the building.

"I've got to say," Donovan began, "I've never before made a woman burst into tears just by asking her to spend time with me."

But he was smiling, which was just what Shayna needed, not his pity. And she started to laugh again. This time, she knew no tears would follow.

"There's a first time for everything," she told him.

"Apparently."

She noticed that Donovan was thoughtful enough to have picked up her tote bag. "Thank you for bringing my bag. What about my nov—"

"Your novel is in there. I figured you were probably through with dinner."

"That was very sweet of you. Thank you." Shayna extended a hand, and Donovan passed her the bag. But then she considered something. "You didn't have dessert. Please, if you weren't finished, we can go back in."

"I don't have much of a sweet tooth. But if you want something…"

Shayna vigorously shook her head. "I'm embarrassed

enough as it is. People are probably wondering what's wrong with me. I'm not normally so…emotional."

"Hey," Donovan said softly. "Don't worry about what anyone thinks. Not even me." He paused. Took a step closer to her. "But if you want to talk, I'm here."

Maybe that was exactly what she needed. She began to walk slowly, and Donovan walked beside her. The building that housed the dining hall was part of the larger hotel structure, around which was a path framed by a stone railing. During the day, the path had shade because it was covered by the floor above it. Now that it was dark, it was a romantic place to walk because of the intermittent lights lining the wall.

"This is supposed to be my honeymoon," Shayna said, then looked at Donovan for his reaction. His eyes widened, but he didn't say anything, so she continued. "I was supposed to get married on Saturday. And I would have if I hadn't caught my fiancé in the back of his car with a stripper."

Shayna kept talking, telling Donovan everything that had happened from that moment on, how she had still gotten dressed up for her big day while Vince hadn't suspected what was going to come next. How her sister had encouraged her to call him out publicly because that was no less than he deserved.

"The last thing I wanted to do was have a quiet talk with him, then have someone announce to everyone in the church that the wedding was off. I wasn't about to shoulder the blame for our failed wedding. People needed to know the truth. And I'll tell you, the satisfaction of seeing him sweat when I dropped my bombshell…" Shayna smiled. "It was priceless."

They were now at the far perimeter of the path, where it abruptly ended. There were steps leading down to the second pool, one Shayna had seen earlier when she'd walked around the resort. And as she'd noticed earlier, this pool area was mostly deserted. The hotel guests tended to congregate around the main pool with the swim-up pool bar.

"Wow," Donovan said. Shayna could only imagine how shocked he was. Here, he'd been probably hoping to strike up an island romance with a single woman—not one who'd had a fiancé only three days ago.

Shayna stepped toward the stone railing and placed both palms on it. She stared out into the darkness, listening to the lulling sound of the waves crashing against the shore.

She sensed when Donovan stepped beside her, feeling his presence. But she didn't look at him.

"So how do you feel?" Donovan asked. "Are you regretting what happened? That you called off the wedding?"

Shayna turned to face him. "Not at all. In fact, I'm thanking God that I found out his true nature when I did."

"Yeah, I can see that. You're strong."

"Strong?" Shayna asked. "You can say that after I fled the table in tears?"

"Of course you're strong. Another woman wouldn't have gone on her honeymoon alone after something like that. She would have stayed home and probably cried the whole week. But by going on your honeymoon alone—and facing what that means—you're trying to get some closure. I admire that."

"Thank you," Shayna said, staring at Donovan in awe. "That really means a lot." Her own family hadn't seen it that way. They'd been worried that she would fall apart on her own, especially in a place where she was supposed to be enjoying her first days as a married woman. But Donovan, a stranger, had realized how vital this was for her in terms of her own closure. And that it showed strength, not weakness.

"Life's not always easy," Donovan said, moving an inch closer to her. "But character is built through the tough times, not the easy ones."

He was different, Shayna realized. Insightful in a way she

hadn't expected. "Are you a therapist?" she asked. "And if so, how much is this going to cost me?"

Donovan chuckled, a soft, warm sound. "No. Not a therapist. Just someone who's gone through some things, so... so I understand."

"Aah," Shayna said. "A woman broke your heart, too."

"Not exactly."

"Oh?"

Now Donovan turned and looked off into the distance. "I was engaged to be married once, too," he said softly.

There was a note of pain in his voice. Shayna held her breath, waiting for him to go on.

"But my fiancée was diagnosed with breast cancer. Ten months before the wedding."

Shayna gasped. She hadn't expected that answer.

"And six months later," Donovan said, facing her again, "she died."

Chapter 8

Shayna's mouth fell open and her chest tightened with pain. "Oh, my God, Donovan. I'm so sorry."

"It's been two years," Donovan said. "And you go on. It isn't always easy, but you do. So yeah, you'll feel emotional sometimes. Laugh when you want to cry, cry when you want to laugh? Absolutely. But you'll…you'll move on."

Shayna's heart ached for him. Suddenly Vince's betrayal seemed very insignificant in the face of what Donovan had lost. She wanted to close the distance between them and wrap her arms around him.

But she stayed where she was.

"I'm sorry," she said again. "I can't even imagine what you went through."

"Thank you," Donovan said. "I only brought it up to say that no matter the pain, time heals all wounds. But I didn't mean to dampen the mood. I'm in a beautiful place, with a beautiful woman…"

Shayna's heart raced at the statement. Maybe it was what

Donovan had just shared, but she was seeing him in an even brighter light. He was gorgeous, sexy as hell, sensitive *and* deep.

Which made him even more irresistible.

Suddenly he covered her hand with his, brushing the pad of his thumb against her skin. It was a light touch that electrified every cell in her being.

"There's a steel drum show starting at the theater in half an hour," Donovan said. "Feel up to watching it with me? After that, if you're up to it, we can hit the disco, which is beside the theater. Music always helps lift the mood."

He was still stroking her skin, and Shayna knew that if she said yes to Donovan, she'd be saying yes to the start of something. Exactly where that would lead, she didn't know.

But despite all reason—and the broken heart she was supposed to be nursing—she wanted to find out.

"Sure," she said. "I'd love to."

Donovan had wanted to kiss her.

The realization had been almost shocking. Not so much because he'd felt the urge but because of how strongly he'd felt it.

It was all he could think about now that he and Shayna had parted ways. She had gone back to her room to freshen up and was supposed to meet him in the lobby in ten minutes.

Why her, why now? Donovan wondered as he paced the marble floor. Why someone who, last week at this time, had been planning to marry another man?

Since Nina's death, he'd thought of dating, and he'd gone out with a few women, but none of them had really sparked his interest. When the last woman he'd gone to dinner with had moved toward him to kiss him, Donovan hadn't pulled back, wanting to see if the kiss would spark an attraction that the conversation with her hadn't.

When it hadn't, he'd found himself wondering if he would ever want to kiss another woman the way he had wanted to kiss Nina.

Now he knew that he did. Shayna, a woman who was dealing with a heart broken by another man, had reignited the passionate fire inside of him.

But instead of kissing her at the moment he'd wanted to, he had touched her hand. Partly to see how he reacted to touching her and also to see how she reacted.

And she *had* reacted. He'd seen her eyes widen slightly and her beautiful lips part. And he'd felt the charge between them, the undeniable pull of attraction.

It was real and it was strong.

Shayna was the first woman since Nina to excite him.

And yet he had refrained from kissing her.

The setting had been right. But the mood hadn't. Not while they'd both been discussing their heartaches.

No, when Donovan kissed her, it wouldn't be at a time when she was feeling sorry for him, nor him for her. It would be when he looked at her and didn't see a hint of any sadness in her eyes.

And he *would* kiss her. Kiss her until she forgot the man who'd been fool enough to let another woman come between them.

Donovan hated cheaters. Despite the entire family's protests, his sister had married a man they knew would hurt her. And he had. The jerk had run after every woman with a skirt. After five years of marriage and three children, Audrey had finally confided in the family that Brad wasn't the husband she thought he would be, that she was certain he'd been cheating on her from the moment they'd said "I do." Audrey had expected her family to riddle her with *I told you so*'s but that wasn't the nature of his family. They were a close-knit group who always supported each other.

So that's what they did when Audrey made the decision to leave Brad. Supported her through the ugly process. Donovan wasn't surprised when Brad subsequently failed to financially support his three children. Now, no one knew where he was. Which was a good thing, because Donovan would probably get arrested if he ever laid eyes on the lowlife. Men who didn't do right by their children were a personal pet peeve of his. His own father had left his mother with three children to raise, not feeling any moral obligation to support his children emotionally or otherwise.

Donovan was there as much as he could be for his nieces and nephews, being the father figure they deserved. He hoped and prayed that one day a good man would come into his sister's life.

But right now, Donovan wondered if it was his time. His time for a good woman to come into his life.

"Hey, you."

At the sound of her voice, he turned. And once again, the mere sight of her had his heart pumping faster.

Damn, she was beautiful. What man in his right mind would sleep with a stripper the night before his wedding and throw away someone as stunning as Shayna?

She was still wearing that gorgeous red dress. It hugged her ample breasts and slim waist and flared out over the hips. She'd added a sweater to ward off the night air's cool chill. Her lipstick was brighter. And instead of the flats she'd been wearing before, she now had low-heeled gold sandals, a dressier look.

Donovan's eyes went to her toes. A white strip was painted across each nail, the same as her fingernails were painted. It was a look he knew was popular these days, and on Shayna it was stunning.

"Been waiting long?" she asked.

"Not at all." She was wearing perfume. Something delicate and floral. Had she put it on for him?

"So," Shayna said, "which way is the theater?"

"This way." Gesturing to the right, Donovan started moving, walking slowly. Shayna walked beside him, and he wanted to slip his arm around her waist and hold her close, but he didn't.

They walked around the front of the hotel, along a road on the hotel's property. When Donovan noticed the lights of a car coming from around the corner, he instantly remembered that cars drove on the opposite side of the road in Jamaica, so he quickly wrapped an arm around Shayna's body and eased her to the side. She stumbled a little from his sudden movement as her feet sought purchase on the concrete ledge, and gripped his shoulders to keep from falling.

And then they stood there for a moment like that, Shayna's hands on his shoulders, his arm wrapped around her waist. She stared up at him, and he down at her. He swallowed, his heart beating fast. This was the perfect time to dip his head and taste those full, sweet lips.

He almost did. Until Shayna giggled nervously and glanced away. "Wow. That was close."

She had to have been talking about the car, but she could have just as easily been talking about a possible kiss. Surely he wasn't the only one who'd felt the moment between them.

She kept walking, not looking at him, and Donovan knew that she'd felt what he had. But she hadn't been ready to take that next step with him. Perhaps she felt she didn't know him well enough. Or maybe she thought that it was too soon to be kissing another man after she'd broken up with her fiancé.

Either way, Donovan was determined to melt her resolve. Because he didn't believe in coincidence. The way he saw it, fate had put the two of them here together on this island for a reason.

He was ready to love again. And some fool of a man had destroyed his chance with Shayna.

Well, that man's loss was Donovan's gain.

Yes, by the end of the evening, he would kiss her. And when he did, she wouldn't want to pull away.

She would want more.

Shayna's body was tingling in places it should *not* be tingling for a woman who'd just ended a relationship. Her mind knew that, and yet her body...

Oh, her body. It seemed to have a mind of its own where Donovan was concerned, reacting with pleasure at the mere sight of him. And when he'd touched her... Oh, boy.

As he'd held her close to him, their faces not too far apart, Shayna had thought he was going to kiss her. In fact, she almost edged her face to his. But she'd suddenly turned away, wondering what in the world she was doing.

The man was practically a stranger. And yet a part of her was attracted to him with a force she'd never truly experienced.

That's it, Shayna realized as she continued to walk with Donovan, neither of them speaking as they headed toward a complex across from the hotel. Shayna could never remember feeling this kind of electric attraction with Vince, not even in the beginning. The attraction with Vince had built slowly, after Shayna had come to see him first as a friend, then as someone with potential. He'd been a man who met all of her criteria and was charming and made her laugh, but she'd never felt this immediate and fierce attraction with Vince.

From her walks to her room from the front of the hotel, Shayna had seen the complex across from the hotel proper, noting that it had a gift shop and medical facility. She could hear the melodic sounds of the steel drums now, so apparently this was where the theater was, as well.

She ascended the steps behind Donovan, and when they reached the top, she saw that they'd stepped into a huge, open area. Shops lined the outskirts of what could only be described as an amphitheater. She'd expected an enclosed structure.

A waitress was passing, and Shayna waved to get her attention. "I'll have a piña colada," she told her. "Do you want another rum punch, Donovan?"

"Actually, I'd prefer a soda. A Coke."

The waitress headed off, and Shayna took an available seat in front of the stage. She was already moving her body to the beat of the steel drums, feeling far better than she had an hour earlier in the restaurant.

And it had everything to do with the man now sitting beside her.

The waitress arrived a few minutes later with their drinks. Shayna already had a little buzz from the drinks at dinner and resolved to drink this one slowly. She wasn't normally a big drinker, but she was in Jamaica with a hot man and was determined to take the edge off her nerves. Nerves that had made her start crying.

No, she didn't want to cry anymore. She was ready to have a good time.

The steel drum performers were outstanding, and after a few songs, people were up on their feet, moving to the lively beat. Shayna leaned close to Donovan and asked, "Feel like dancing?"

Before he could answer, she was on her feet, swaying her hips from side to side, letting the music flow through her. Donovan was right. The music was lifting her spirits, soothing the wound in her soul.

And so was Donovan.

Shayna looked to her right. Donovan wasn't on his feet. Instead, he was patting his hand on his thigh in time to the music's beat.

And watching her dance.

Shayna saw heat in his gaze, and that heat seared her skin. A delicious thrill shot through her. The thrill that came from a man's eyes riveted to her every movement.

She felt very much a woman, sexy and desirable. One who was flirting with a man who would send most women's libidos into overdrive.

The song finished and people clapped. Then another peppy song began. Shayna reached for Donovan's hands. "Come on," she said. "Dance with me."

He grinned at her as he rose to his feet and joined her in the aisle. She swayed her hips in time with his, watching every seductive movement of his body. Her eyes traveled over his strong thighs, up his flat belly and to those muscular arms. Second to a great smile, Shayna loved muscular arms.

Maybe it was the alcohol, but she found herself leaning forward and touching his biceps. They were as hard as rocks. She knew she was flirting, sending out a sexual signal, and yet she couldn't stop herself.

I really like your arms, she thought.

"You do, hmm?" Donovan asked. "Years of working out."

Oh, dear God. Had she spoken her thought aloud? Yes, the alcohol must have been getting to her.

In fact, her head swam a little, and she gripped Donovan's arms to steady herself.

"You all right?" he asked.

"Actually," she began, "I think I should sit down."

Donovan placed a hand on her back and guided her to the nearby seat.

Shayna sat, but her head suddenly felt heavy, and she realized sitting wasn't the best option. She needed to be on her feet, letting the cool breeze help sober her up. "Actually, I think I'd be better off taking a walk."

"And some water would be a good idea."

Shayna placed her hands on her hips and gave Donovan a look of mock reproof. "Are you saying I'm drunk?"

"I wouldn't say drunk," he began diplomatically. "But… happy."

Shayna laughed at that. She *was* happy. She definitely wasn't about to burst into tears again.

"My goodness," she said, "what do they put in those piña coladas?"

"Rum. Probably a lot of it."

Shayna giggled again. "You can hardly taste it. But then, bam! It sneaks up on you."

Donovan grinned, and Shayna thought fleetingly that he was chuckling *at* her because she was talking too much, but she was beyond caring. She asked him, "Will you walk with me?"

"Of course."

She started in the direction of the steps they had come up. "I want to go to the beach," she announced. "I've never walked on a beach at night."

"Never?"

She shook her head. "Well, not a beach in the Caribbean."

"Then, lovely lady, you're in for a treat."

As Donovan met her eyes, an undeniable jolt of heat passed between them. Earlier, Shayna had turned away when she thought Donovan might kiss her. But if the opportunity came again—*when* it did—she wouldn't turn away.

Because she was ready to see where this attraction with him would lead.

Very much so.

Chapter 9

"Let's go," Shayna said. She giggled and began a sort of skip-shimmy movement toward the steps, moving to the music. Donovan watched her, smiling. Oh, yes—the alcohol had gotten to her. But it had helped turn her into a happy drunk, unlike some people he knew who became depressed when they drank too much.

He trotted to catch up with her. "Hey, Shayna."

She whirled to face him, still moving that delectable body of hers to the steel drum beat. "Hmm?"

"Wait right here. Let me get that water for you, okay?"

"Oh." She didn't stop moving. "Right."

Her happiness was infectious, even if fueled by rum. He wondered if she had any clue just how sexy she was.

Donovan walked quickly to the nearby bar, got a bottle of water, then returned to Shayna. She was still moving, unashamed to be dancing on her own.

As she neared him, she gyrated that sexy body of hers in front of his, raising her hands in the air as she did, inviting him to dance. And damn if his groin didn't fill with heat. She was smiling up at him, looking so full of life and fun, Donovan found himself wondering again why any man on earth would let someone like her slip from his grasp. It was impossible to resist her invitation, so he moved his hips in front of hers, getting close but not touching her. Because if he touched her...

He didn't want to embarrass himself. He was a man, after all, and his body was reacting to the sumptuous woman in front of him.

But it wasn't just her physical attributes. Yes, she was gorgeous, but it was more than that. Something about her spoke to him on a primal level he didn't understand.

And what he knew of her character, he loved. The fighting spirit. The decision to leave her fiancé at a point that had to have been excruciatingly hard. To come to Jamaica alone spoke to the strength of her character.

"Whoa," Shayna suddenly said, stopping. She placed a hand on her forehead. "I think I need to slow down."

"Here." Donovan opened the bottle of water. "Drink some water."

She did, downing several gulps. Which was good. She needed the water to counteract the alcohol.

Sweat glistened on her brow. She'd wiggled and shimmied and gyrated until she'd broken out in a sweat. Exhaling heavily, she pressed the cold water bottle to her forehead. "Ooh, that's better, but I definitely need to walk on the beach now. Feel the cool breeze on my skin."

He wanted her to feel something else on her skin. His lips.

But of course he didn't say that. Didn't even make a move to touch her. She was past tipsy and might easily respond, but that wasn't how Donovan wanted to experience their first kiss. He wanted her sober and willing.

He started down the stairs, and she moved with him. Once on the sidewalk, they turned left, heading toward the beach.

The sounds of the steel drums could still be heard, and Shayna continued to sway her body gently to the music. Within moments, they were passing a playground, and beyond that was the sand.

Shayna ran toward it, giddy with excitement. "The beach at night!"

Stopping on the sand, she slipped off her sandals and held them in one hand. Then she stared ahead of her, as if in awe.

Donovan came to stand beside her.

"Listen to that," Shayna said, turning to him. "Nothing but us and the ocean. It's incredible."

You're incredible was the thought that popped into Donovan's mind.

"The world is so big and beautiful. So many different experiences. So many other cultures to explore. This is my first time leaving the States. But it makes me want to see as much of the world as I can."

Nina had had the same wish. To travel to every continent. They had planned, for their honeymoon, to go to Ghana, where Nina's grandparents had been born.

Donovan inhaled deeply, expecting to feel the customary sadness that came with thoughts of Nina. But instead of the sharp stab of pain, he felt a dull ache. The sadness was still there but nowhere near as intense as it had been before.

Instead, what he felt as he watched Shayna dig her toes into the sand, was hope.

How was it possible that someone he'd just met was making him feel a sense of hope for the future?

"I thought the steel drums sounded incredible," Shayna began, "but the sound of the ocean at night…it's music all its own."

And then she started swaying her hips again. Slowly. Seductively. Either the alcohol was fueling her movements, or she was deliberately being provocative.

Either way, as Donovan watched her, he wanted her with a fierceness that surprised him.

Maybe Shayna sensed the direction of his thoughts, because she turned suddenly, her smile bright as she regarded him. "Come here!" she called. "I just saw a crab."

"A crab?" Donovan asked as he walked toward her.

"It went in the sand right there," she said, pointing.

Donovan followed the direction of her finger, and indeed, there was a hole in the sand. "Maybe you ought to put your shoes back on," he told her. "You don't want to get your toes bitten."

"Oh, they have more reason to fear us than we do them," Shayna stated matter-of-factly.

No, of course she wouldn't want to put her shoes back on. A woman who had stood up to her fiancé in front of countless wedding guests wouldn't be afraid of a few crabs in the sand.

That was one way she differed from Nina. Nina would have likely been screaming by now at the sight of the crabs, clinging to him for support. Shayna, on the other hand, was clearly used to standing up for herself.

"You probably think I'm crazy," Shayna said, "being so excited to be on a beach in the Caribbean."

"Not at all," Donovan told her. "It's charming."

Shayna turned around again, facing the dark ocean. She walked toward it, not stopping until her feet hit the water. She walked along the water's edge, occasionally digging in her toes.

Donovan stood back, watching her. Because if he approached her now, he wasn't sure he could refrain from drawing her into his arms and kissing her. He wanted nothing more.

But he wanted it when she was completely sober.

"Come," she called out to him, extending her hand.

So Donovan strolled toward her. She kept her hand outstretched, and as he got within reach, he took it.

They walked hand in hand for several seconds, with the lights of the resort to their left and behind them and nothing but the black ocean to their right. How was it that they were so comfortable while hardly knowing each other at all?

It didn't matter how. It only mattered that it was. Once again, Donovan took their easy rapport as a sign that fate had brought them together.

Suddenly Shayna stopped. Moaning, she put a hand against her forehead.

Donovan instantly moved in front of her, taking hold of her by her upper arms. "Are you okay?"

"Yeah," she said after a moment. "But I think... I think I should probably lie down."

"Let me get you back to your room."

Shayna's eyes widened as she looked up at him.

"Just to make sure you get there okay," Donovan assured her.

"Of course," she said softly.

"Which building are you in?"

"The one right there, at the very end." She pointed to the last building that was near the beach and the casual beachfront restaurant.

"Nice and close," Donovan said. "That's good."

They began to walk in that direction, Shayna leading the way. When he saw her visibly shiver, Donovan didn't think—he just slipped his arm around her waist and snuggled her close.

It was a brazen move, but she didn't pull away. Donovan

had the feeling that for her, as for him, there was a comfort level. It was effortless and natural, as though they'd been dating for years. Once again, Donovan couldn't help feeling that fate was at play, bringing them together at this juncture in both of their lives.

The delicate scent of her perfume floated on the air, and Donovan found himself wishing he could dip his head to her neck to really inhale the alluring scent. To kiss her smooth skin.

"You're a gentleman," Shayna said quietly when they reached the stone path beyond the sand. Her building was directly in front of them. "Thank you for being so sweet."

Donovan's heart thundered in his chest at the comment. Was that a brush-off? "The you're-a-nice-guy" kiss of death?

"I'm going to see you to your door." The very thought that she might be seeing him as a friend disturbed him. Far more than it should. "Which way?"

"Upstairs."

She walked ahead of him into the building, then went down a hall and around a corner to get to the stairwell. She didn't slip back into her shoes as she climbed the three flights of stairs.

He felt an odd rush of uncertainty. Or perhaps just nervousness. Was Shayna sobering up and distancing herself from him? He wasn't sure.

Donovan could only imagine his brother and cousin having a laugh at his expense if they knew what he was thinking. They'd tell him he'd forgotten how to gauge a woman because he'd been out of the game for so long.

But when Shayna got to a door and turned to face him, he knew that his momentary anxiety had been uncalled for. She looked up at him and grinned a sly, flirty smile.

"I had a very good time," she announced.

He saw the rise and fall of her chest, and knew that she was also nervous. "I did, too."

"Thank you for getting me to my room safely."

"Of course."

Shayna paused, and he saw her gaze darken. Saw her lips slightly part. She wanted him to kiss her.

And man, he wanted that, too.

But he'd already made his decision. The first time he kissed her, she would be sober. The last thing he wanted was for her to wake up in the morning and have any regrets.

But mostly, he wanted to leave her wanting more.

"Well," Shayna said, and sighed. "I guess that's it. For now."

"I'll see you tomorrow."

Shayna stared up at Donovan, her chest rising and falling rapidly. The way he looked at her... His heated gaze made her feel incredibly alive. Desirable. And that was exactly what she needed right now.

She also needed something else. After the walking on the beach, the holding hands, she wanted a little more. A little taste of the fantasy.

He stared down at her and she back at him. As his eyes focused on her lips, she flicked out her tongue, moistening her skin. She kept her lips parted in invitation, wanting him to kiss her.

But when he didn't kiss her, Shayna frowned.

"Good night, Shayna," Donovan said.

Good night? That was it? After setting her body alive with that slow, hot gaze of his, he wasn't going to kiss her?

"Oh, gosh," Shayna said suddenly, understanding. "You must be thinking that I'm some sort of alcoholic."

"No, that's not what I'm thinking."

"Are you sure?"

"Yes. I'm very sure."

Shayna eyed him warily. "Then what *are* you thinking?"

"Honestly?"

"You can be honest," she said, fueled in part by her tipsy state. "I can take it."

"Honestly? I'm wondering how any man could ever let you go." And then his eyes moved slowly over her from head to toe, leaving Shayna's body flushed.

Surely he would kiss her now. Surely. Her heart began to race, and she held her breath in anticipation.

And when Donovan began to lower his head to hers, Shayna closed her eyes and sighed.

But instead of feeling his mouth on hers, his lips brushed her forehead. Shayna waited…but nothing.

Her eyes popped open. Donovan was grinning at her.

"Good night," he said softly.

"G-good night?" Shayna stammered.

"Yes, good night. Get some rest. I'll see you tomorrow."

Shayna frowned, wondering if Donovan was serious.

"Where's your room key?"

"It's right here." Shayna dug into her purse and withdrew the card key.

Donovan took it from her fingers and proceeded to open the door. Though Donovan had said good-night, Shayna's pulse began to race. Was he going to walk her into the room, kiss her there?

He pushed the room door open while still standing outside, making it clear he wasn't going to enter.

"Go ahead," Donovan said.

Reluctantly, Shayna stepped into the room. Almost immediately, she whirled around to see if Donovan was still there. But he was already walking away.

She watched him. After about ten steps, he turned around. "Good night, Shayna," he said again. With a wink, he added, "Sleep tight."

Chapter 10

The next morning over breakfast, Donovan was aware that his sister kept giving him odd looks. He was directly opposite her at the large round table in the dining hall, the kids between them on his left, and his brother, sister-in-law and their two children on his right. His cousin and wife hadn't yet made an appearance. They were either running late or skipping breakfast.

"Okay, kids," Audrey said. "Hurry up and finish eating. We've got to get back to the room and get ready for our trip."

The family was going on an ATV tour and then to a place called Island Village, a theme park where they would enjoy a variety of water sports as well as other activities and entertainment. Donovan had been looking forward to the trip, but now he'd had a change of heart.

"About today's excursion," Donovan began, "I'm gonna pass on this one."

"What?" Audrey asked, her eyes meeting his from across the table. "But you've already paid."

"It's okay," he said. "I'm not big on ATVs. And the Island Village will be nice, but hey, I've got the beach here. I feel like chilling at the resort today."

There was that look from his sister again. The look that said she knew there was something he wasn't telling her.

He couldn't blame her. The excuse he'd given sounded lame to his own ears.

Beside him, Antwon elbowed him. "Chill, huh? Is that code for something else?"

"Something like wh—" Audrey asked. And then her eyes lit up with understanding. "Oh, I get it. It's that girl, isn't it? The one you went to have dinner with last night. You've made a love connection!"

"I haven't made a love connection," Donovan said, trying to be cool.

"I wondered where you were last night after dinner," Audrey went on, a grin on her face. "You were with her!"

"He was walking on the beach," Lynda said, her eyes lighting up with a knowing look.

Donovan's eyes shot to hers, shocked.

"We've been waiting for you to tell us all about her," Lynda went on.

"Walking on the beach?" Audrey said.

And at the same time, Antwon said, "Looks like our little brother's found someone who sparks his interest."

"We saw them from the room," Lynda said in response to Audrey. "They were holding hands."

Everyone exploded in chatter. Donovan held up both hands, saying, "Please, everyone. Settle down."

"Settle down?" Audrey said to him, her face beaming. "You met someone you like and you expect us to calm down? Tell us all about her!"

Donovan should have known that he couldn't keep any friendship that might develop here a secret, but he was stunned at the keen interest in everyone's eyes. With the exception of the kids, his family was looking at him as if he had just won the lottery.

"Yes," Lynda crooned. "Tell us about her. Because obviously you really like this one."

"Lawd, it's about time!" Audrey exclaimed.

Donovan stared at his sister, saying pointedly, "You're getting ahead of yourself."

"Bro, we saw the two of you walking on the beach last night. Looks like whatever's going on with this one is moving very fast."

No chance of keeping his interest in Shayna quiet. Even the newlyweds had probably heard about it. Probably even his aunt and uncle, who had opted to stay at a different resort nearby.

"Next time I head to Jamaica, I'm going by myself," Donovan quipped.

"What's her name?"

Donovan's eyes went to Clay in surprise. At nine, he was the oldest of his nieces and nephews, but he hadn't expected him to be at all interested in this conversation.

It was clear his family wouldn't let up until he gave them answers. They were that kind of family. Large and loving. And very involved in each others' lives.

"Her name is Shayna," Donovan said slowly.

"Shayna!" everyone exclaimed, and Donovan had to chuckle.

"And where's she from?" Lynda asked.

"Buffalo, New York."

"Not too far from Maryland," Audrey piped in. "They've got flights from BWI direct to the Buffalo Niagara International Airport."

His sister was already mapping things out. "Yes, I know that. I used to fly Southwest to visit Tony in Buffalo all the time."

"Go on," Audrey said, missing the hint of playful sarcasm in his voice.

"What else do you want to know?" Donovan asked.

"Everything!" Lynda and Audrey replied in unison.

Donovan chuckled. *Women*. They lapped all this stuff up.

But even Antwon was regarding him with anticipation.

"Here's something interesting," Donovan began. "She was supposed to be on her honeymoon this week."

"Honey*what?*" Audrey asked, frowning.

"Uh-oh." This from Lynda. "Who dumped whom?"

"She caught her fiancé with someone else the night before their wedding," Donovan explained. He lowered his voice. "One of the entertainers from the bachelor party."

"Damn," Antwon said.

"Hmm, she might not be ready to move on," Audrey surmised.

"I don't agree," Lynda said. "If she was all torn up over the guy, she wouldn't come to the place where they were supposed to honeymoon. That'd be too painful."

"Yes," Audrey agreed, nodding. "You're right."

"And she must have been the one to call the wedding off if she caught him cheating," Lynda added.

"Good for her," Audrey commented. "Another woman might have married him anyway, hoping he would change." She rolled her eyes. "I should know."

Donovan watched the women, fascinated with how they were assessing the long-term prospect of a future between him and Shayna.

Damn, he really had been single a long time for everyone to be so excited at the thought that he'd met someone.

"Since you're all so interested," he said, "she confronted him at the altar, in front of all their guests. Then she broke it off and came to Jamaica anyway, trying to move on."

"She's definitely moving on," Antwon said, a smile playing on his lips.

"What does that mean?" Donovan asked.

"Come on, bro. Walking on the beach with you, hand in hand…"

"You think it's too soon for her?" Donovan asked, feeling suddenly uneasy. "That maybe she's on the rebound?"

Antwon shrugged. "Naw, I'm not saying that."

"And maybe she already knew this guy wasn't right for her, but catching him cheating made that very clear," Lynda offered. "When a woman's done, she's done."

"You know that's right," Audrey agreed. "Might take them a long time to get to that point, but when they do, it's like turning off a switch. One minute they're in love, the next they're ready to open their hearts to someone new."

Donovan's stomach eased, the responses making him feel a lot better. Because he didn't want to think that any interest Shayna showed might be a rebound attraction.

And again, he was shocked that he cared that much.

"We're developing a friendship," Donovan said. "We'll see how it goes."

"We might end up seeing very little of you, little bro," Antwon said, chuckling. "The way we're hardly seeing Stefan and Ophilia."

"Damn, you all are putting me on the spot," Donovan said. "I'm just getting to know this girl. We're not honeymooning like Stefan and Ophilia."

Audrey wiped Avery's mouth, her youngest child at five, then suddenly said, "What does she do?"

"I don't know. I didn't ask her."

"Shayna…" Audrey's eyes suddenly narrowed. Then they widened. "Wait a minute. *Shayna*."

"What?" Donovan asked. "What does that mean?"

"I wonder…" Audrey went on, but she didn't finish her statement.

"Wonder what?" Donovan asked anxiously.

"No, it couldn't be," Audrey said to herself. Then, "But what if it is?"

"You've completely lost me, sis."

"You know how I'm always reading," Audrey said.

"Yeah?"

"Well, there's an author I love to read. Her name is Shayna Kenyon. She writes really fabulous historical romances. I wonder… I wonder if she could be *that* Shayna."

"A romance writer?" Donovan asked doubtfully.

"Why not?" Audrey countered. "They go on trips, too. Get married, too. Get their hearts broken."

He supposed his sister was right. It was possible. Anything was possible. But he doubted it.

"Ask her," Audrey said. "When you see her today. Ask her if she's Shayna Kenyon and if she writes historical romances."

Donovan shrugged. "Okay. I'll ask her."

Lynda looked at her watch. "We've got to go, everyone. We have about half an hour to get to the room, get our stuff and then get back to the lobby for the bus."

There was a flurry of activity as everyone stood. Only Donovan stayed seated, taking another sip of his coffee. There was no need for him to rush.

Audrey came around the table and slipped her hands around his neck from behind. She kissed his cheek. "I'm glad you met someone," she told him. "And if it's Shayna Kenyon…" She let out a little squeal.

Antwon patted his brother's shoulder as Audrey eased back. "Have fun *chilling,* bro."

"Tell her we want to meet her," Lynda said.

"I'm not sure about that," Donovan said, but he was joking. "You all might be a little too much a little too soon."

Audrey's hands went to her hips as she stared at Donovan. "Donovan Deval, if you don't bring her to us, we'll all come to you."

Donovan knew it was true. That's the way his family was.

"If she's still interested in talking to me, you'll all see her later," Donovan explained.

"Why wouldn't she be interested?" Audrey asked.

"We've got to go," Lynda said, tapping her watch. "We'll have to have this conversation later."

Audrey, Antwon and Lynda rounded up the kids, said their final goodbyes and started out of the restaurant.

When Antwon was near the door, he turned and gave Donovan a thumbs-up.

They were all so hopeful.

Donovan could only hope that in the light of day, after sobering up, Shayna would still be interested in pursuing a friendship with him.

Who was he kidding? He wanted more than a friendship.

A lot more.

The first thing Shayna was aware of when she woke up was her pounding head.

Then she remembered the previous night. The drinking. The dancing. The walk on the beach.

The chaste good-night kiss on the forehead.

No, it wasn't a chaste kiss, Shayna thought. *Not in the least.*

It had been a soft, lingering, seductive kiss on her forehead, the kind meant to leave her hot and flustered and wanting more.

And it had worked.

Because she *was* thinking about him. She remembered her movements in front of him last night. How she'd been dancing. Flirting. Even though she had been drunk, she had known what she was doing.

There was no doubt that she was fiercely attracted to this man. But it simply didn't make sense. Not for someone who, just last week, had been in love with someone else.

But with the alcohol weakening her inhibitions, she had allowed herself to show a flirtatious side. She was willing, at least with the aid of some piña coladas, to see just how attracted Donovan was to her.

Had it been a kind of game? Maybe something to help make her feel better in the wake of her heartbreak?

But if that been the case, wouldn't she now be regretting the way she had walked on the beach with him, asked him for his hand, and looked up at him with eyes that surely had to have said "kiss me now"?

The truth was, she didn't regret any of it. And that in itself was baffling to her.

But why should it be baffling? Donovan was gorgeous, clearly the type of man a woman would fantasize about. In the wake of her failed wedding, she simply needed a diversion. Something to take her mind off all that had gone wrong.

That diversion was a six-foot-two man with smooth skin the color of milk chocolate, a washboard stomach and muscles in all the right places.

At least Shayna was smiling. She could very well be spending this very moment depressed. Or curled up with a book. Not that she had anything against books but it was nice to want to get out of the room. To not feel that her only way to escape sadness was to lose herself in a fictional world.

Shayna stood, stretched, then headed for the bathroom.

That's when she noticed the slip of paper on the floor near the door.

She went to it, bending to lift it, wondering if the hotel had sent her some kind of message. She opened the folded paper and read.

Shayna, I hope that you slept well.
I had a wonderful time with you last night.
I look forward to seeing you again today.
Donovan

Her lips erupted in a grin. It was more than a simple note. It showed just how thoughtful Donovan was, to head all the way back to her room to slip it under her door, knowing she would see it when she awoke.

It was like flowers after a first date, letting her know that he was interested in spending more time with her.

And despite all reason, Shayna wanted to spend more time with him, too.

Very much.

Chapter 11

Shayna saw Donovan immediately. He was sitting in the spot where they'd been the day before, the comfy lounge chairs beneath the straw umbrella.

Earlier, she had gone onto her balcony and looked down to see if she could spot Donovan on the beach. She hadn't been able to, and assumed—rather, hoped—that she would find him by the pool, which she was not able to see from where her balcony was positioned.

He didn't see her right away. But she knew the moment he did, because his back went a little straighter, then a smile formed on his lips.

It was nice. More than nice, really. To see his reaction at seeing her lifted her spirits instantly.

"Thank you for the note," Shayna said to Donovan as she reached him.

He gestured to the seat beside him, upon which was a folded towel.

"Is that for me?" Shayna asked, referring to the towel.

"Yes," Donovan said. "I was hoping you would join me."

Shayna sat, noting that only Donovan was here today, not any of his family members. Then her eyes ventured back to Donovan, who was looking incredibly fine in black swim trunks. His abs had to be more than a six-pack. More like eight.

"How're you feeling today?" Donovan asked.

"Actually, I'm not feeling too bad." She paused. "I took some Advil."

"Ahh." Donovan nodded. "Smart move."

"So, how long did it take you to get to my room to leave me that note?" The resort was huge, and Shayna had no clue where Donovan's room was. The walk could have been endless.

"Just under two hours," Donovan said, grinning. "But you were worth it."

She laughed. A heartfelt laugh that expressed her true feeling of joy. When she'd seen Vince in the car with that stripper, she couldn't have imagined that she'd be laughing so heartily days later. That another man would be making her laugh.

"I'm glad you're laughing. After what you told me..."

"About the wedding that never was," Shayna supplied, knowing that he hadn't wanted to say it. He probably didn't want to upset her by bringing it up again.

Donovan nodded. "Yeah. I'm just thinking that it's nice that you're not feeling sorry for yourself."

Shayna offered him a small smile but said nothing. Instead, she looked around. "So, where is everybody? Your family, I mean?"

"Off on some excursion."

"And you're not with them?"

"I told them I wanted to relax today."

Even through his dark sunglasses, Shayna could see that his eyes were holding hers. And she got the distinct impression that he had deliberately skipped out on this particular excursion so that he could be with her.

"Are you sure that's why?" she asked him. "Or did you stick around to make sure I didn't have alcohol poisoning?"

Now Donovan was the one to throw his head back and laugh. The sound was warm and infectious. She started to chuckle, as well.

"You're funny," he told her. "Really funny. But no, I didn't stick around to make sure you didn't have alcohol poisoning." He paused, and again she could feel the intensity of his gaze. "I stayed today because I want to spend more time with you."

Shayna's stomach fluttered with the simple admission. She couldn't deny it made her happy. And not just because she'd have company for the day.

"Thank you," she said. She set her bag behind her on the chair. "I appreciate that."

"Do you have a book in your bag?" he asked her.

"Actually, I left my books upstairs. Based on your note, I figured I'd find you here."

"*Books?* You brought more than one?"

"I'm a fast reader. And since I figured I'd be spending the week by myself, I could easily get through four or so."

"You like reading," Donovan said.

"That's an understatement. I own about a million books. So yeah, I'm a big reader."

"Hmm." Donovan nodded, seeming to consider something. "Okay, I have something to ask you."

"Sure," Shayna said, sensing something in his tone.

"Now, this might sound a bit crazy. But when I told my sister your name was Shayna, she asked me to ask you if there's any chance you write novels. Apparently, she's read some books by a Shayna Kenyon, and since the name isn't that common…" Donovan shrugged. "Crazy, huh?"

Shayna didn't respond. She was too stunned to speak. Donovan's sister had recognized her as a writer?

"Whoa," Donovan said, apparently figuring out by her nonresponse that his sister had been correct. "Are you Shayna Kenyon? Really?"

She hadn't planned to come out and tell him what she did, but there was no reason to deny it. "I'm in shock. No one has guessed who I am just by my first name."

Donovan sat up. "You're Shayna Kenyon?"

"Yes. I'm Shayna Kenyon. Romance novelist."

"Damn." Donovan chuckled. "My sister is gonna freak out."

"She's read my books?" Shayna asked, a little in awe.

"Of course she's read your books. She does nothing but read. With three kids, I don't know how she has the time, but she's always buying books."

"Bless her heart," Shayna said proudly.

"You say you've got a million books. My sister probably has five million. Romances are her favorite."

"And what about you, Donovan? Have *you* read any romances?"

She'd been joking as she asked the question and figured she'd get the typical male response to the "Do you read romance?" question. She expected an eye roll at the very least, and possibly the "those books are for women" reply.

But Donovan said, "I haven't, no. But now that I've met you, I will definitely read yours."

Score another point for Donovan. While Shayna didn't expect anyone to read her books, she'd been disappointed that Vince had shown no interest. He'd always laughed off her suggestion that he read any of her novels, claiming that those novels were strictly a woman's domain.

"Wow," Donovan said, shaking his head as he smiled. "I

can't believe you're a romance writer. A writer, period. And that my sister knows who you are."

While Shayna was proud of her work, she wasn't particularly the type of person who wanted to be the center of attention. So she changed the subject. "What about you? What do you do, Donovan?"

"I own a few retail stores."

"Oh? What kind of stores?"

"Clothing. Urban clothing. A friend of mine and I decided to open the first store because we thought it would be something fun to do. Now, we've got three stores. All in Laurel and the surrounding area. We made a conscious decision to hire at-risk youth. Kids who might not end up on the right path because they're in a tough neighborhood. My friend Alan and I both benefited from a Big Brother program—our fathers weren't around—and we wanted to do something to help give back."

Shayna stared at Donovan with a renewed sense of awe. He was truly incredible. Based on what he'd just told her, it was clear that he was a kind and considerate and thoughtful person. It was harder to not like him.

"That sounds amazing. What are your stores called?"

"Street Sense," Donovan replied. "The clothes are hip, the kind of thing young people can be proud to wear. And because we offer opportunities to the youth in the community to work in the stores and even submit designs, it's become very popular. For me, it's given me a sense of purpose. If I'm helping keep a few kids off the street, then that alone makes me happy."

"That's wonderful," Shayna said. "Truly inspiring." And if she wrote contemporary romances, she would certainly write about someone like him. Perhaps she would have to craft a character based on him anyway. She'd come up with something.

"How old are you?" she asked him suddenly.

"Thirty."

She nodded. "You're very…mature. I like that."

"How old are you?" Donovan asked.

"Older than you."

"No, you're not."

"Yes, I am."

"Really? You don't look more than twenty-six, twenty-seven."

"Well, I'm thirty-two."

"You *are* older than me," Donovan said.

"Is that good or bad?" Shayna asked, eyeing him warily.

"It's all good, Shayna. I like older women."

He winked at her, and then a heated look passed between them.

After a moment, Donovan said, "Have you eaten yet?"

"No, not yet. I came to find you first. Have you eaten?"

"I ate with my family before they left for the day. But I'm happy to go with you to the restaurant. We can leave our towels here, to keep our chairs."

"Sounds like a plan," Shayna said.

Donovan stood and, to Shayna's chagrin, he slipped a T-shirt on. Which only made sense since they were going to the restaurant. But Shayna so admired looking at his body that she preferred to see him with his shirt off.

He met her gaze suddenly, and Shayna knew that he'd caught her brazenly checking him out. She should have looked away…but she didn't.

Instead, she let her eyes continue to roam over his magnificent physique—letting him know without question that she liked what she saw.

After eating breakfast, Donovan and Shayna swam in the pool for a little bit before Donovan suggested that they head to the beach. "Over there, we can get in a paddleboat or a canoe. Do something a little different. If you want."

"If I get in a canoe, my paddling skills are so bad I might end up in Mexico," Shayna joked. "But a paddleboat sounds fun."

"Oh, I wouldn't let you end up in Mexico."

"You don't know my canoeing skills."

Donovan chuckled softly. Together, they made their way to the large inlet. On one side were the canoes and boats. Within minutes, they were in a paddleboat, both peddling away on the calm water.

They marveled at the colors of the ocean. At the beautiful shoreline. They splashed each other. And they laughed. A lot. Shayna was amazed not only at their easy rapport but at the definite chemistry between them.

There wasn't a point when she thought that she needed some time to herself. Time to just relax on her own. And that surprised her.

After about an hour of paddling, they both decided to take a rest. The water had been calm, thankfully, so they'd been able to go out a good distance without fear. It had been Shayna, Donovan and the Caribbean Sea. And Shayna knew that she could have stayed out there with him much longer.

She just wanted to be near to him.

As they returned the paddleboat, Shayna wondered about the feelings she was having for Donovan. She was attracted to him physically, yes. She could understand that. But she was making a deeper connection with him, as well. An emotional one. Was it simply a coping mechanism for her? A way to help her deal with Vince's betrayal?

"Feel like heading into the water to swim?" Donovan asked. "I like the pool, but nothing beats the ocean."

"Sure."

They walked along the sand past the boats to the stretch of

beach where people were lying on chairs and splashing around in the water. As Shayna had noticed from her balcony the first day, people were a good distance in the water without it being past their waists.

After placing her bag and their towels by a chair, she started into the water with Donovan. It was clear and beautiful. She walked at least twenty feet and the water only came to her knees. But the moment it got a bit deeper, she began to swim.

She didn't realize Donovan was swimming beside her until she stopped and felt his arm go around her waist.

She righted herself, wiped at her wet face. Then looked up at him and saw undeniable heat in his eyes. Her stomach fluttered.

"What are you thinking?" she asked him, her voice soft and low. Seductive.

"Just how beautiful you are."

Shayna's heart began to pound. Like last night, she wondered if Donovan would kiss her.

But unlike last night, a doubt popped into her mind. She moved backward, away from his touch.

"What's the matter?" Donovan asked.

"Nothing."

"No, that's not true. Something is bothering you."

Shayna sighed. "It's just—"

But she didn't finish her statement, and Donovan wondered what had happened to make her withdraw. Because that was what she'd just done.

"You can tell me," Donovan said.

"It's just weird, that's all."

"What's so weird?"

"You. Me."

"You mean both of us here together?" Donovan asked. "Instead of you and your fiancé?"

"Sort of."

Shayna had moved away from him, but Donovan closed the distance between them once more. He didn't want her thinking about her fiancé. So he snaked his arms around her waist. Skimmed the damp skin of her back with his fingers.

He wanted to make her forget the fiancé who had not been worthy of her.

And in his heart, he believed that she wanted the same thing, too.

He pulled her close to him, holding her gaze. Her eyes widened slightly. Not just with surprise but something else.

Desire.

"Oh, boy," she said.

"What is it?" Donovan asked softly. "What are you thinking?"

Her breasts were pressed against his body, and he felt her shuddery breath. "I'm not sure I should say what I'm thinking."

"Go on," Donovan urged.

"If you want to know the truth, I'm thinking about last night." She glanced away for a moment, then looked up at him again. "I remember being on this beach last night. And I remember very much how I wanted you to kiss me."

"And?"

"And…" A frown marred her beautiful face. "It makes me wonder—considering I was drunk—how different that makes me from Vince? Vince was drunk and he messed around with that stripper. If I were to kiss you last night, so soon after Vince…"

"But you didn't."

"No, *you* didn't. You didn't kiss me."

Though she hadn't phrased it as a question, Donovan knew she was asking one. "Why didn't I kiss you?" he said. When she didn't speak, he went on. "Because I didn't want you to have any doubts. I didn't want you to think that the alcohol had made you do something you didn't want to."

She nodded. "I understand. And that was the right decision. Because I would have wondered."

Donovan slowly trailed his hands up her back. Anyone watching them would think they were a couple. A happy couple on a honeymoon. Or together on a romantic vacation.

"What about now?" Donovan asked. "What are you feeling now? Now that you haven't had anything to drink? Do you still want to kiss me?"

Shayna's eyes widened slightly. And again, her breath swelled beneath her breasts. God, he wanted to dip his head to her neck and kiss the flesh there.

"Yes," she said, her voice a whisper. "I do."

Her words surprised her. She had mentioned last night not just to gauge where Donovan's head had been but to examine her own thoughts. She could easily have dismissed a kiss with him the previous night as too much alcohol influenced by a romantic setting. But now...

Donovan's arms tightened around her. And then his head began to lower toward hers. She tilted her own head back. Closed her eyes.

And unlike last night, Donovan's lips did not land on her forehead. They brushed against her own lips, soft and oh so sweet, eliciting a moan from her immediately.

His mouth moved over hers, and she parted her lips. And when his tongue entered her mouth, the reaction was more potent than any of the alcohol she had consumed the night before.

She felt heady, her knees weaker. She gripped Donovan's strong biceps, holding on to him and not wanting to let go.

All too soon, the kiss was over. She moaned in protest.

And when she opened her eyes and looked up at Donovan, she saw that he was smiling at her.

"Kissing you now," he began, "I know that your reaction is real. Not a result of clouded judgment." Donovan paused, then said in a lower voice, "I want to kiss you again, but not here."

But not here... The very thought that Donovan might want to kiss her somewhere else, like behind closed doors, made Shayna's center throb.

How could she even be considering such a thing? Let alone wanting it?

Because she did want it. In Donovan's arms, she wanted the entire fantasy. The fantasy that started with hot glances and deep kisses and ended with making love.

Shocked at the direction of her thoughts, Shayna stepped out of Donovan's arms. And then she dove into the water again. But the Caribbean Sea couldn't wash away the lustful thought that popped into her mind.

Chapter 12

Later, Shayna and Donovan were sitting at the beachside casual restaurant. He had a burger and fries on his plate, while Shayna had opted for broiled fish and French fries.

She was curious about Donovan's late fiancée. Curious about how their relationship had been. A perfect fairy tale gone wrong? Or an imperfect relationship? Was he still grieving the loss of this woman?

"So," Shayna began, "I've told you all about Vince. Do you feel like talking about your fiancée?"

Donovan swallowed his mouthful of food, then spoke. "What would you like to know?"

"How long did you date?"

"A little over four years."

"That's a long time."

"I know. But Nina and I didn't want to get married until we were ready—both financially and mentally. Some of our friends married young, and they broke up. My sister had gone through a particularly nasty divorce. We knew if we loved each other waiting wouldn't matter."

Shayna nodded. "How long did you know her?"

"She was my college sweetheart."

The admission made Shayna's mood fizzle. And she didn't know why. What should it matter if Donovan and Nina had been in love since kindergarten? The woman was no longer here.

Shayna knew the answer to her question. She liked Donovan. And instead of thinking realistically—that this relationship they were building was one that would last on this island only—she was letting her mind venture into territory it shouldn't.

"I can't even imagine what it must have been like to lose someone you loved like that."

"It was devastating," Donovan said candidly. "I didn't know if I could go on. But each day, little by little, the pain subsided. I never imagined that it would, but it did."

Shayna wondered how a person dealt with that. Especially when they dared to love again. Was there a measure of guilt they felt at falling for someone new?

Falling for someone new…? Why was Shayna even letting her mind go there? If anything happened between her and Donovan, it was going to be a casual island fling. It was ridiculous to even think of anything else.

"I haven't dated," Donovan said. "I haven't wanted to." He paused. "Until now."

Despite her thought just a moment ago, Shayna felt something inside her come alive at Donovan's statement. Was that what they were doing? Dating?

No, they definitely were not dating. They were enjoying each other's company. She had suffered pain. He had suffered pain. They were two souls coming together at a time when they needed each other.

"I don't want to scare you," Donovan began. "But I mean that when I say it. Until now, I haven't even considered dating anyone. Well, that's not true. I have considered it. But no one has interested me. I think my family was starting to worry about me, worry that I was too lost in my grief to meet someone else I liked. Even I worried about that. But meeting you…" Donovan's voice trailed off.

"Meeting me what?" Shayna asked.

"You're different," Donovan said simply. "I enjoy spending time with you." He shrugged. "Who knows?"

Who knows what? Shayna couldn't help wondering. She wanted to ask him that, but didn't. It was fairly obvious what he was getting at. That perhaps something might spark between them.

Something already *had* sparked between them. But Donovan almost sounded as though he wondered if that something might lead beyond their time on the island.

It didn't surprise Shayna. She could tell he was a serious guy. A devoted type of man. Dedicated and strong. Honorable. He probably didn't engage in casual relationships.

"I'm glad I met you, too." Shayna smiled. "Honestly, you helped make this trip so much better for me already."

"When I mentioned Dunn's River Falls yesterday," Donovan began, "I could tell it upset you."

There was no point in denying it. "That's because my fiancé and I discussed going there. I had checked out the pictures online, saw how breathtakingly beautiful the place was. And it made me sad for a minute. Made me realize how everything in your life can change in a heartbeat. But I don't have to tell you that."

"No, you don't. But I can also tell you, having met you, that I know things can change in a heartbeat for the better."

Donovan stared at her intently, not breaking their eye

contact for several seconds. He was making it clear to her, with that look, that he was seriously interested in her.

Maybe he was ready for that. Finally ready to date again, to move on beyond his pain.

Was Shayna?

"I'd like for you to go to Dunn's River Falls with me tomorrow," Donovan said. "As you said, it's a beautiful place. The kind of place to take someone special. I'd like to take you."

Shayna's breath caught in her chest. No doubt about it, Donovan was letting her know he was interested. And as much as a part of her wanted to tell him that she didn't want anything serious, that she knew nothing serious could come of this sort of island flirtation, she couldn't. Because in her heart, she wanted to spend more time with him. He was exactly the kind of man who could dominate her fantasies. And it was hard to say no to that kind of man. Even if she didn't want to let herself believe that they could ever have anything real outside of this magical place.

It had only been two days, after all.

Two days and a fierce attraction to him that she could not deny.

But reason got the better of her and she said, "Donovan, I don't know…"

"Don't know what? Whether or not you want to get to know me a little better?"

Oh, she definitely did. That was not the issue. "It's just…I don't know if I can trust what I'm feeling."

"And what are you feeling?" Donovan asked.

Damn, that was not what she'd meant to say. How on earth had that slipped out of her mouth? She hadn't meant to talk about any feelings for him. And yet she had, as though another part of her—a part she clearly could not control—was leading her actions and words.

Was that what was going on? Was her grief causing her to act completely out of character?

It didn't feel like that. Because the truth was, she really wasn't thinking about Vince. Wasn't pining over their break-up.

"What are you feeling?" Donovan asked again.

"I'm feeling very attracted to you," Shayna admitted. Once again, she was startled at her words. Why was she telling this man her innermost feelings? This wasn't how flings were supposed to go. Flings were supposed to be based on a hot attraction to each other and perhaps a lot less conversation than they were engaging in.

Their bodies were supposed to do the talking.

"And I'm attracted to you," Donovan said. "Something is happening between us Shayna. And I'm not afraid of it. Are you?"

"I…" She halted, unable to go on.

"Don't say it's too soon," Donovan said, his voice husky. "Don't be afraid to give your heart again."

That sexy voice… It washed over her like warm rain. And it made her want to feel the deep timbre of that voice whispering in her ear.

Shayna had barely eaten her food, but she pushed her plate aside. She wasn't hungry anymore. At least not for the kind of food that filled one's belly.

"Feel like going for a walk?" Donovan asked.

She should say no. She should stop whatever it was that was happening between them. Because her rational brain knew that it would not last. In the way she suspected that Donovan did not have casual relationships, she wasn't one to have them either. So what was the point in even continuing to spend time with him here? Getting involved would certainly lead to pain.

That was her rational thought. But the irrational was

overwhelming all reason. The irrational had her saying, "What did you have in mind?"

"The truth?"

With that simple question, Shayna saw a heat in his eyes that spoke volumes.

"I want to be somewhere with you where there aren't so many eyes around," Donovan said.

The man was irresistible. There was no denying that. Her attraction to him was growing more and more each second.

Was it just lust?

Shayna still said nothing, just stood. Donovan stood, too. And when he reached for her hand, she didn't pull away.

They strolled along the stone path beneath where her balcony was, walking back toward the center of the resort. She thought Donovan might lead her toward the pool. Instead, he crossed the rocky inlet, heading in the direction of the gazebo.

"This is where my cousin and her husband got married," Donovan explained. He pointed toward the gazebo. "It was absolutely beautiful. It made me think, that if I were to ever get married, this would be a perfect spot."

Shayna could honestly say that she'd never met a man quite like Donovan. He was romantic at his core. She could see that now. Romantic and intense and passionate and hot. He had the kind of intensity that might scare many women away. And yet she wasn't running.

"Have I upset you?"

Shayna's eyes flew to Donovan's. "Why would you ask me that?"

He shrugged. "It just occurred to me how mentioning a wedding might affect how you're feeling."

And the truth was, Donovan had also asked the question because he wanted to feel her out. He wanted to see how she would react to talk about a wedding. He liked her. A lot.

But the reality was that she had just gone through a sudden breakup. Did she see him only as a man who was making her forget about her pain?

Because that was not what Donovan wanted to be to her.

He wanted to be everything to her. And he didn't know why. But his attraction to Shayna was fierce and inexplicable and real.

So fierce that it *should* scare him.

And yet he wanted to embrace it with abandon. Throw himself one hundred percent into what he was feeling for Shayna.

Was that crazy? He didn't know. But something in his soul told him it was right.

"No," Shayna said. "It doesn't upset me. In fact, I'm a little bit surprised by that. And maybe I'm even feeling a little bit of guilt."

"Guilt?"

Shayna nodded. "Yes. Because I shouldn't be feeling as happy as I am now. My fiancé just broke my heart. And yet, it's almost like I've all but forgotten him. How can that be possible?"

"Because maybe in your heart, you knew the relationship wasn't right."

Still holding her hand, Donovan led her to the railing of the gazebo overlooking the sea. He leaned his hip against the white railing and faced Shayna.

"Why would you say that?"

"It's just a feeling, Shayna. You said it yourself. You're not really thinking about him. And I understand the desire to move on, especially given that he hurt you, and yet you and I… There is no denying we have made some sort of a connection. Is that the kind of connection you could make if your heart truly was with your ex?"

"I—"

Donovan didn't let her finish speaking. Because being this close to her, away from prying eyes, he could no longer hold back. He slipped one arm around her waist, pulled her close and kissed her again.

He kissed her to quell any of her protests. He kissed her to show her that what he was saying was true. He kissed her to make her forget her crazy ex-fiancé once and for all.

And damn if she wasn't soft and sweet and completely irresistible. She sparked something in him the likes of which he wasn't sure he'd ever felt before.

Not even with Nina.

She moaned against his lips, and her hands went to his shoulders. He deepened the kiss, delving his tongue as far as it could go, twisting it with hers. She dug her fingers into his skin, which only urged him on. He pulled her closer, flattening her full breasts against his hard muscles. He wanted to feel those breasts with his hands. To make her melt with his tongue and his touch. He wanted to see just how explosive it would be between them.

The thought made him hard.

Shayna broke the kiss and stepped backward. He looked down at her, at her eyes that had darkened. Darkened with the desire she felt for him.

"Tell me now that you could kiss someone else like that if another man was in your heart," Donovan said.

Shayna's entire body was tingling with a sexual fervor. She was hot from head to toe.

Hot for Donovan.

And she realized that he was absolutely right.

"Oh, my God," Shayna uttered.

"What?" Donovan asked. "What is it?"

"You're right," Shayna said softly. "I never connected the dots, but I can see it now."

Donovan stared at her, waiting. When she didn't continue, he said, "What do you mean by that?"

"My sister was the one who suggested we should go to where the guys were having the bachelor party," Shayna explained. "See what they were up to. And I realize now that I wanted to go because I wasn't sure what I would find. Maybe on a subconscious level, I *expected* to find something out of place. But if I had totally trusted Vince, I would not have gone. I would have known that he would never get out of line." Shayna looked away, out at the vast sea. "I never realized that until right now."

Donovan stood behind her, wanting to touch her but not doing so. This wasn't the right moment. This was a time for her to evaluate something she had just discovered about her relationship and perhaps herself.

Turning, Shayna looked up at him. He could see the pain in her eyes. "I never truly trusted him. Not that I expected him to cheat on me, but obviously somewhere in my heart I knew. I *knew*."

"And how do you feel about that?" Donovan asked.

"I don't know," Shayna said. "I loved Vince. But maybe I loved the idea of him more than I actually loved him. I would have been faithful to him," she went on, stressing that fact. "Put everything I had into the marriage. But maybe it would have been to the wrong man." She paused, adding almost in a whisper, "Even if he hadn't cheated on me."

Now, Donovan placed his hands on her shoulders. He wanted to support her through whatever it was that she was feeling.

"I don't understand." She shook her head. "It's not like I got involved with him and had my head in the sand. I cared about him. Until last week, I thought I loved him."

"And I'm sure you did love him. But like you said before—it

was better that you find out now that he was a man unworthy of you."

"You seem to be very in tune with women. You just got me to open up, to see things in a different light. How did you do that?"

"I'm the youngest," Donovan explained. "I have two older sisters, a mother, a host of aunts and for a while two of my female cousins even lived with us. I got my training on how to deal with women." He smiled.

It was such a charming smile, a smile that had disarmed her, a smile that had helped her to open up. Shayna found that she suddenly wanted her lips on his again. So she was the one to lean forward this time, tip up on her toes and press her mouth to his.

As she did, she sighed. And with that sigh went the last of any thoughts about Vince.

The last of any guilt.

She was embracing something new and enjoying every moment of it.

Chapter 13

"As much as I've enjoyed spending all day with you," Donovan began hours later, "I'm going to have to meet my family."

He and Shayna were standing on a path near the pool, and he was running the palms of his hands up and down her arms. He didn't want to leave her, but he also knew that there was something to be said for the art of the tease. Something to be said for letting two people who were falling for each other miss each other for a little while.

The old adage rang true: absence did make the heart grow fonder. And just thinking of not seeing her for a while was already making him miss her.

"Of course," Shayna said. "I don't want to keep you from your family all day."

"They've been busy without me," Donovan explained. "But knowing them, if they don't see me soon, they're liable to start their own brand of espionage to see what I'm up to."

Shayna regarded Donovan suspiciously. "Hmm. Sounds like there's a story there."

Donovan raised his eyebrows. "Apparently some of my family members saw us last night. Walking along the beach. You can imagine the conclusions they're coming to. And when I told them I wasn't going to go with them today..."

"More fuel to the fire," Shayna supplied.

"Exactly. You're welcome to join me for dinner with them. I'm sure they wouldn't mind."

"Thank you, but no," Shayna said. "I would feel very uncomfortable. Maybe *very* is too strong a word, but I'm just getting to know you and..."

She let her voice trail off, not finishing her comment. But Donovan was also feeling the same way. He knew that at some point on this trip Shayna would meet his family. Maybe even tomorrow if she decided to go with them on their excursion to Dunn's River Falls, but for now he didn't mind keeping this day as strictly theirs.

"Do you think you'll go with us tomorrow to Dunn's River Falls?" Donovan asked.

Shayna began to nod slowly. "Yes, I think I might like that."

The answer pleased Donovan. Because this time, he didn't see any hint of guilt or sadness in her eyes at the mention of going to Dunn's River Falls. He saw only a woman who wanted to spend more time with him.

"I guess I'd better go upstairs to the lobby and buy my ticket." Shayna looked in the direction of the steps that led upstairs to the terrace.

"Actually..."

Again, Shayna looked up at him with curious eyes. "Actually what?"

"I took the liberty of buying your ticket earlier this morning. Before you met me at the pool."

"You did?"

"Yes."

"But what if I hadn't wanted to go?"

"Then that would have been okay," Donovan said. "That's why I didn't tell you until now. I didn't want to influence your decision. But I was hopeful that you would say yes."

He was also hopeful of something else.

Of the fact that he would end up in her bed.

Because for the first time since Nina's death, Donovan wanted a woman. In that complete way that a man and woman were meant to share each other, please each other.

It might seem inconceivable to feel so strongly for Shayna in such a short time, but he did. And he wasn't going to question it. He believed in fate. And he believed wholeheartedly that fate was at play here.

Given the way the day had gone, he would be surprised if Shayna wasn't thinking about the same thing. That at some point they would end up in bed.

But Donovan was not into casual hookups, especially not the kind people engaged in to pass the time on vacation. As much as his body wanted to connect with Shayna in that most primal of ways—wanted it badly   just like the kiss, he did not want to rush into bed. He wanted to build what was growing between them. And again, he wanted to leave her wanting more.

The time would come when they would explore their passion to the fullest. And when it did, Donovan was determined that the experience would be one unlike any Shayna had ever experienced before.

Shayna left Donovan downstairs outside of her building. She went up to her room on her own, not having any concerns for safety in the daylight. She also felt that Donovan was content to give her a kiss downstairs because he didn't want to do so outside of her bedroom door. The chemistry between them could not be denied forever, and if he walked her to her room and kissed her there, that might just prove to be too much temptation.

Shayna liked that he was clearly thoughtful about these things. But she could also see in his eyes that he was as hot for her as she was for him. She knew he was exercising a lot of restraint in not pushing for things to go further faster. And she was grateful for that.

In the hallway outside of her room, there was a large opening in the wall where a person could look down to below. Several such openings were placed strategically along the floor's halls, positioned where windows would be. A good four and a half feet up from the floor, people could rest their arms on the ledge and look outside.

It was on the path below that opening where Shayna had kissed Donovan goodbye. She went to it now and peered outside on the off chance that he was still standing there. She wondered if he, like her, wanted that one last glimpse.

A smile warmed her from head to toe when she saw Donovan standing on the path by the hedges. Seeing her immediately, he raised his hand in greeting. Giggling, Shayna waved back.

And then she heard the sound of footfalls on the tile floor behind her. She whirled around, suddenly afraid.

And when she saw who was standing behind her, she gasped in fear.

"Hello, pretty lady."

A cold chill washed over Shayna. Seeing Garth standing there scared the life out of her. Where had he come from?

For some reason, Shayna's eyes went to her door. It was slightly ajar. She most definitely had *not* left it that way.

Quickly looking through the opening to downstairs, Shayna hoped she would see Donovan. But he was gone.

No one else was around. At least she couldn't hear anyone in the hallway.

Garth took a step toward her. "I've been waiting for you."

"Were you in my room?" Shayna asked, her brain already scrambling for a way to escape the situation. She knew that her sixth sense about Garth had been dead-on.

There was something off about him. Something she could not trust. But the question was, could she trust him not to hurt her?

"I wanted to see you," Garth told her. "Ever since I met you, I haven't been able to stop thinking about you."

Perhaps the only way Shayna was going to get away from this man was to cause some sort of a scene. To be loud enough that someone would come to her aid.

"Were you in my room?" she demanded again, this time more loudly.

Garth stepped toward her. Shayna hugged the wall and sidestepped him. She hoped that would be the end of it, that she would be able to get to her door and slip into the room. But no such luck. Garth darted out a hand, ensnaring her arm.

"I just want to get to know you better," he said. "Let me help you forget the man who broke your heart."

"I want you to leave me alone," Shayna said firmly. She tried to squirm out of his grasp, but he didn't release her.

Instead, he brought his mouth down onto hers.

Shayna tried to scream, then did her best to push him away from her. But he was too strong. Too overpowering.

He pushed her toward her room door, and Shayna knew that once he got her inside things would get a lot worse.

But suddenly, Garth was releasing her. Impossibly, *he* was being pulled back.

But how?

And then Shayna saw Donovan. He had Garth by the collar of his shirt, and the next instant he slammed him against the wall. He didn't even give the man a moment to speak before he punched him in the face.

"What the hell are you doing?" Donovan yelled. "Attacking a woman?"

Garth fought back not by punching Donovan but by squirming and pushing him off him until he was free. And then he took off down the hallway, sprinting away as fast as he could.

Donovan went to Shayna immediately, gathering her in his arms. "Are you okay?" He framed her face. "Did he hurt you?"

"I'm fine," Shayna said, breathing heavily. "How did you—"

"I knew something was wrong when you suddenly looked around," Donovan explained. "I got up here as fast as I could."

"He works at the hotel," Shayna said. "He's a bellman. He took me to my hotel room the first day and he seemed a little too into me but I never thought he would—" Shayna stopped, realizing the gravity of the situation. What would Garth have done if Donovan hadn't shown up?

It was that thought that had the tears flowing from her eyes. The knowledge of how close she'd come to being violated by someone.

Donovan framed her face and wiped at her tears with the pads of his thumbs. "It's okay now," Donovan said. "I'm here now."

"I want to go in my room."

"Of course." Cradling Shayna in his arms, Donovan led her into the room. He brought her to the bed where he set her down.

Shayna continued to cry softly, though Donovan could tell she was also trying to compose herself.

"I think he was in my room waiting for me," Shayna said. "I'm not sure why he came out. Maybe he heard me in the hallway. But suddenly he was there, and my door was slightly open, and I just *knew...*" Stopping, she gazed up at Donovan, her eyes wide with horror. "What if you hadn't shown up when you had?"

"Shh." Donovan sat on the bed beside her. "You can't let yourself worry about that. Don't worry about what could've happened. I'm here. And while I'm here with you, I won't let anyone hurt you."

Shayna believed him. Not only was he gorgeous and sensitive, he was strong. The kind of man who would do whatever it took to protect his woman.

"We're going to have to go to the manager," Donovan said. "Tell him what happened. Do you know this guy's name?"

Shayna nodded. "Yes. His name is Garth."

"Good. I know you might not be up for it, but we should do this now."

"You're right. Let's call now. I don't want Garth hurting anyone else. And what he did to me... He can't get away with that."

Donovan stood and went to the phone in the room. He made the call to the front desk. And when the manager came on, he explained what had happened.

Moments later, Donovan hung up the phone and rejoined Shayna on the bed. "The manager is on his way to the room. Given the sensitive nature of the situation."

"Good. Yes, it's better that he come to me." Shayna paused as she faced Donovan. "Will you stay with me?"

"Of course I will."

He took her hand and held it in support, and with that touch, Shayna felt better already.

* * *

The manager arrived a short while later, as did hotel security. In the privacy of Shayna's room, she was able to explain to them everything that had transpired with Garth. From their first meeting to the uncomfortable feeling she got from him while heading to dinner to him having entered her room to wait for her.

According to the hotel manager, Garth was nowhere to be found. After Donovan had fought him, he had taken off and was likely not going to return. But they would find him at his home residence and have him arrested.

"If you would like to press formal charges—"

Shayna didn't let the manager finish his statement. "No. I don't want to press formal charges. I'm only here for five more days, and I don't want the headache of giving a statement to the police. All I really want is to make sure he stays away from me. I don't want to see him again." Shayna felt a pang of anxiety rush through her. Deep down she knew she should have Garth prosecuted, but the thought of a long, drawn out trial was too daunting.

"I don't believe that will be a problem," the manager said. "If Garth shows up to work again, he will immediately be escorted off the property. In the meantime, we would be happy to move you to another room as a precaution to ensure your safety."

"That's a great idea," Donovan said.

"Yes, that's a great idea," Shayna agreed.

They moved her to the floor below, the room directly beneath her current one. Another honeymoon suite that had recently been vacated.

Donovan helped her move her belongings and get settled in. And only after he was certain that she was one hundred percent settled and safe did he tell her he was going to leave.

"If you want to come with me to dinner, it can be just the two of us," he suggested.

"No," Shayna said, shaking her head. "I'm not hungry."

"Are you sure?"

"Yes, I'm sure. Besides, I don't want to take you away from your family."

"Don't worry about that, Shayna. Not in the least."

"I'm really not up for it," Shayna said. "I'm going to spend a quiet evening in the room."

"Do you still feel like going to Dunn's River Falls with me tomorrow?"

Shayna couldn't spend the rest of her vacation locked up in a room in the hopes that she could escape a crazy person. "Definitely," she said. "We're still on for tomorrow."

And then she smiled and slipped her arms around Donovan's waist. "Thank you again for a lovely day. And thank you for being here throughout this ordeal."

Donovan gave her a soft kiss on the lips. Not the kind of kiss to ignite any fires within her but a kiss of support. The kind of kiss that assured her he was there for her.

Again, it was just what she needed.

Donovan started for the door. "If you need anything, just call me." He gave her his room number. "Even if you just want to talk."

"Okay," Shayna said softly.

"Otherwise, I'll see you in the morning."

Donovan opened the door and glanced into the hallway, as though making sure no one suspect was around. Satisfied, he turned back to her. And then he dipped his head for another soft kiss.

Reluctantly, Shayna eased back. "See you in the morning."

"Close your door," Donovan said. "And bolt the lock."

She gave him a wave before doing so, then rested her shoulder on the wooden door once it was shut.

And despite the ordeal with Garth, she was smiling.

Because she was starting to feel that Donovan had come into her life for a reason. One that was all good.

Chapter 14

The next morning, Shayna's phone rang bright and early. At first she was alarmed. She didn't want to answer it in case it was Garth. But then she remembered that she was in a new room, and Garth would not know where she was. And it might've been Donovan calling to check on her.

It turned out that it was the hotel manager on duty for that morning, calling to assure her that Garth had not returned and that in the interim the police had gone to his house to give him a stern warning. There was no chance that Garth would be coming back to the resort as he'd been fired, so Shayna had nothing to worry about.

That was welcome news for Shayna, a huge burden off her shoulders. She could go about enjoying the rest of her week without worrying that Garth might appear.

And the rest of the week included Donovan.

Or did it?

She suddenly realized that she hadn't asked him when he would be leaving. She was here until Sunday and had assumed that he would be, as well. She'd already imagined spending each of those days with him. The realization that maybe that wouldn't be the case had her feeling a little out of sorts.

She was attracted to him and knew she wanted to take things to the next level. But there was a timetable for whatever might happen between them. It was Wednesday. What if he was leaving tomorrow? She didn't want him to leave before they had a chance to make love.

She was beyond being surprised by the direction of her thoughts. It was something she had considered the very first moment he kissed her. Before that, really. She had thought about the possibility of sharing Donovan's bed practically from the moment she had learned that he wasn't married.

A fling. As her friends would call it—a palate cleanser. Something to firmly get the taste of Vince out of her memory.

It was so unlike her to consider sleeping with a man after knowing him barely two days, but the pull of attraction between her and Donovan was undeniable. As crazy as it was, as out of character as it was, she knew she wanted him in her bed.

Whether or not it actually happened remained to be seen.

Shayna chuckled at that thought. Who was she kidding? She and Donovan were going to spend more time together, and at a place as romantic as Dunn's River Falls, their attraction was sure to grow.

So was the temptation.

Before coming on this trip, Shayna had assumed that she would spend all her days quietly reading and enjoying the scenery. Gaining perspective. She never contemplated that she would be in the position to even *consider* an affair.

And yet, she was doing exactly that.

Perhaps the bigger shock was that she didn't regret the thought. Not in the least.

Whatever happened today, she was going to enjoy her time with Donovan. She would put no limits on what could happen between them.

With that thought in mind, she showered and slipped into her sparkly gold two-piece, a bathing suit she hadn't yet worn on this trip. Checking herself out in the mirror, she smiled. The bikini was sexy as hell and looked amazing on her.

Donovan would like this one.

Very much.

She put a black shift dress over the bathing suit and gathered her belongings. And then she left the room, ready to embrace whatever the day had in store for her.

When Shayna saw the woman heading straight toward her, her gait strong and fast, alarm shot through her. *Who is this woman and what does she want with me?* Was it someone from the hotel who wanted to talk to her about Garth?

It took her about another second to recognize the woman as one of the people from the group with Donovan.

"Shayna," the woman began, her eyes lighting up. "Shayna Kenyon?"

It was Donovan's sister, Shayna realized. Had to be. She relaxed. "Yes. Are you—"

She didn't get to finish her thought because the woman immediately wrapped her in a bear hug and squeezed her hard. "Shayna Kenyon! My goodness!"

"You must be…" Shayna's voice trailed off. It occurred to her that she didn't know Donovan's sister's name. So she finished, "Must be Donovan's sister."

Releasing her, the woman pulled back and beamed at her. "I've read all your books! And girl, that last one, set in Africa…I totally fell in love with Kwame."

"Thank you," Shayna said. "He was one of my favorite heroes to write. What's your name?"

"My brother didn't tell you?" Her eyes went wide. "I'm Audrey."

"Well, it's very nice to meet you, Audrey. I'll be sure to get you a signed book when we get back home."

"I would love that."

Shayna looked beyond Audrey to the rest of the group. The children were all there, as were the other women and men. But she didn't see Donovan.

"Looking for Donovan?" Audrey asked. "He just went to get some water."

"Ah."

"Well, come on over," Audrey said. "Meet everyone."

Shayna was a little nervous. It felt weird to be meeting Donovan's family, as if she and Donovan were an item. But she was going with them all on the excursion to Dunn's River Falls, so now was as good a time as any to get introduced.

She walked across the lobby with Audrey to the rest of the gang, where she met Antwon and his wife, Lynda, the cousin Dennis and his wife Lorraine.

"And this is my cousin Ophilia and her new husband Stefan." Stefan looked Hispanic. Or perhaps East Indian. Whatever he was, he was extremely attractive. "They've decided to leave the room to spend some time with us," Audrey added, smirking.

"Very nice to meet you," Shayna said, shaking their hands.

She was introduced to the children. Audrey's were nine-year-old Clay, six-year-old Tamara and five-year-old Avery. Antwon and Lynda were parents to seven-year-old Isaiah and three-year-old Sheree, the young girl Shayna had helped out of the pool. Five-year-old Keira was the only child of Dennis and Lorraine. Only Clay, the oldest of all the children, seemed particularly interested in Shayna. He'd been alternately playing a Nintendo DS and giving her surreptitious glances.

He looked up from his game when Audrey said, "Clay, can you believe this is Shayna Kenyon? She's one of the authors I love to read." Again, she beamed. "I can't believe we're in Jamaica at the same time, at the same resort and that you've become friends with my brother."

"Are you my uncle's new girlfriend?" Clay asked.

Shayna's eyes widened at the same time that Audrey exclaimed, "Clay!"

Clay shrugged. "I was just wonderin'. You guys were talking about it at "

Audrey clamped a hand down on Clay's mouth, then forced a laugh. "Don't you mind Clay."

Shayna wondered what Donovan had said about her. But not for long. Because he suddenly appeared, crossing the lobby from a hallway that was near the terrace. And Lord if he didn't look like a vision.

He was wearing denim shorts that were frayed at the hems and covered him to midthigh. On his upper body, he wore a white muscle T-shirt. Shayna's eyes were drawn to his powerful-looking thighs and then higher, to his arms. The sleek, dark sunglasses he wore made him look all the more attractive.

Whenever he was within her sight, Shayna wanted to touch him. He had that kind of body.

Audrey must have realized that something had caught her eye, because she turned, following Shayna's line of sight. And then she grinned. "Oh, there's Donovan now."

Shayna actually had to lick her lips as he neared, realizing that her mouth had gone dry. He was a mix of strong and gentle, which was what was so damn appealing. He had shown that strength yesterday when he had so decisively taken care of Garth. He'd shown the gentleness afterward in her room as he'd held her in his arms while she cried.

If he were gorgeous, muscular and stuck-up, he wouldn't have interested Shayna at all.

Audrey hurried to her brother, and Shayna forced herself to look away. She had to play nonchalant. Not make it so darn obvious that she was in lust with the man.

"We've met Shayna," Shayna heard Audrey crooning. Shayna was about to turn and formally greet him, but before she could, she felt familiar hands on her waist. Instantly, she felt a flush of heat.

While holding her from behind, Donovan kissed her cheek. A casual gesture men had done to women since the beginning of time, she was sure, but to Shayna, it was far from casual. For her, it spoke to the intimacy she and Donovan had already developed.

"See," Clay said, a confused look on his face, "she *is* Uncle Donovan's girlfriend."

Audrey smiled awkwardly. Donovan released Shayna asking, "What did I miss?"

"Nothing," Shayna said, saving Audrey from having to explain away anything. "I met your family, and they're lovely."

Stefan was holding Ophilia from behind, much the way Donovan had been holding Shayna a moment ago. Their bodies swayed gently to a beat shared only between the two of them.

It made Shayna think of her and Vince, how they might be here right now if she hadn't caught him cheating on her. Would he be holding her the way Stefan was holding Ophilia, the two of them so in tune that they moved their bodies to a beat shared between them alone?

She doubted it. Vince had never been the most romantic man

in the world, even though she'd considered him a good catch. They would be reserved with their emotions in public.

As she continued to watch the natural romance and affection between Ophilia and Stefan, she realized anew that that's what had been missing in her relationship with Vince. The passion.

Maybe, ultimately, the love had been missing.

Oh, she'd loved him, but not with the kind of passion she'd written about in her books. The all-consuming passion that drew two people together with a force of its own.

The kind of passion she was feeling for Donovan.

"If you're going to Dunn's River Falls, please have your tickets ready," a man announced. "I will be coming around to collect them momentarily and give you your wristbands, which will give you access to the falls."

Donovan slipped his hand in hers. And that simple touch ignited the burning fire within her for this man. It was something that Vince's touch had never been able to do.

Holding her hand, he gently urged her to walk a few steps to the side with him. When they were out of earshot of the family, he looked at her with concern and asked, "How are you?"

Shayna realized he was referring to how she was dealing with what had happened the night before. "I'm good," she said softly. "Thanks to you."

"Do you know if Garth came back to the resort?"

"The manager called bright and early this morning. He told me that Garth did not return, but that the police went to his home to give him a stern warning. I'm not worried about him anymore. I think he'd be crazy to show back up at the resort. He's not going to want to get arrested."

Donovan framed her face. "Good. I'm glad we don't have to worry about him."

We. It wasn't lost on Shayna that he had spoken about Garth as if he was *his* problem, too, not just hers. The way a husband or boyfriend might.

Donovan leaned his lips close to her ears and said, "So what did you think of my family? Too much?"

"Not at all," Shayna said. "They're lovely." And she meant it. She could tell they were a loving and lively group. "I hope they don't feel like I'll be stealing you away from them, going on this trip with you."

"Are you kidding?" Donovan said. "They're thrilled. My sister is one of your biggest fans."

"Oh," Shayna said. She'd been certain that Donovan had been about to give a different reason for their being thrilled.

"And—" he nuzzled his nose against her cheek, not at all hiding his affection for her "—they're very happy I'm spending time with you."

And then he kissed her. A soft peck on her lips that lingered for a full four seconds.

"I'm glad you're coming with me," Donovan said softly.

Damn, if he kept touching her like this, giving her soft kisses and using that bedroom voice on her, she was going to tell him they ought to skip out on the trip altogether and head straight to her room.

"What are you thinking?" Donovan asked.

"Nothing," Shayna lied, turning so he wouldn't see her smirk. There was no way she could share her racy thought with him. Though maybe he'd already seen the proof of her thought in her eyes.

"Tickets?" a man said, and Shayna and Donovan produced theirs. He put plastic wristbands on their arms, and then they were free to get on the bus.

Donovan took her hand again, and Shayna linked her fingers with his, embracing this man who was her island fantasy come to life.

However the fantasy played out, she was ready for it.

Chapter 15

The trip from Runaway Bay to Ocho Rios did not take long. Less than half an hour. Shayna and Donovan sat at the back of the bus, holding hands the entire time. Before them, Donovan's newly married cousin and her husband also sat holding hands. It wasn't lost on Donovan that he seemed to feel as much attraction to Shayna as Stefan did to Ophilia.

He would never tire of touching her. And even something simple like holding hands had him wanting to kiss her senseless. And thinking of kissing her stirred within him a raging desire that was hard to control.

"This place is beautiful," Shayna announced once they were through the entrance and walking on the Dunn's River Falls property. They were surrounded by beautiful bushes and lush foliage but nowhere did Donovan see any falls. There were many vendors selling various locally made crafts and T-shirts, among other things.

The tour guides from the bus had advised people to stay together as a group. They would even climb the falls holding hands, which Shayna had seen pictures of online. That was apparently a popular and fun way to climb the falls. For those who didn't want to stay with the group, they were given the time to return to the bus.

Given that Donovan's group had children, they decided they would take their time and climb the falls on their own.

Audrey said, "Oh, look. There's a place where you can rent or buy water shoes."

"Good idea," Lynda said.

The tour bus driver had also explained that the rocks they were going to climb today could be slippery at parts and that renting or buying water shoes was a smart idea.

Shayna, Donovan and the family made their way over to the hut where the water shoes were being rented and sold, and after spending a good fifteen minutes getting everyone outfitted, they were on their way along a sloping path that led downward. A man with a donkey adorned in colorful flowers and a straw hat was offering to take photos of the children with the donkey for a fee. Audrey and the other parents decided to stop with the kids to get that cute photo op. Donovan and Shayna continued on.

"This place really is quite stunning," Shayna said, looking around.

"And we haven't even seen the falls yet," Donovan said.

Stefan and Ophilia were strolling in front of them, hand in hand, enjoying the view and each other. It made Donovan want to exhibit the same level of public affection for Shayna. He was holding her hand, yes, but he wanted to wrap his arms around her, hold her close to his side and show her exactly how he was feeling for her.

What *was* he feeling? It was a question that had popped into his mind several times last night. He had lain awake thinking about what he might have done to Garth had he actually hurt Shayna.

All that thinking had proven one thing. Just how much he had come to care for Shayna in such a short time.

The walk down to the beach took a good ten minutes at a fairly brisk pace. Donovan and Shayna had lost the rest of the family members. They would no doubt meet up with them again at some point, but Donovan certainly didn't mind being alone with Shayna.

On the beach, there was a hut and a woman renting locks for lockers where they could put their belongings. Donovan paid for a lock, and then he and Shayna chose a locker nearby.

If Donovan had thought Shayna breathtaking before, as she pulled her black dress over her head and revealed her gold bikini, his libido went into overdrive. She looked absolutely stunning. His eyes traveled over her full breasts, that hourglass waist and shapely hips.

Good Lord, she was a vision of pure loveliness.

Donovan turned, knowing that he would find all the men in the vicinity were checking Shayna out. And he was right. Men blatantly ogled her.

As long as they stayed away, they could look all they wanted. After all, who could blame a guy for being unable to take his eyes off someone as beautiful as Shayna?

Facing her once more, Donovan let his gaze roam lazily over her from the top of her head to her toes. He drank in every luscious curve of her body. The gold bikini complemented her caramel skin and was more than eye-catching. It had him thinking of getting her naked.

He blew out a low whistle. "Damn, you look absolutely amazing."

"Thank you." Shayna looked up at him coyly and placed her hands on her hips. She did a little twirl, nice and slow. She knew exactly the effect she was having on him.

Donovan wanted to gather her in his arms and take her behind one of the sprawling palm trees and have his wicked way with her. Kiss her and touch her until she was screaming his name.

"Look at you," Donovan said. "You're like a little sex kitten."

"Sex kitten?" Shayna said, laughing.

Donovan slipped an arm around her waist and pulled her against him. "Yeah," he said hotly against her ear. "It's going to be very hard to keep my hands off you."

"Who says I want you to?" And with that, she raised her eyebrows in a flirtatious challenge.

"Oh, it's like that, is it?"

Her reply was an airy laugh. And then she began to walk along the sand toward the mouth of the falls. A number of people had gathered there, some beginning to climb, some standing in the water at the base taking photos.

Her behind was round and perfect, and Donovan looked at it shamelessly for several seconds. The bikini bottom had strings at the side that were tied in bows. All he could think of was how easy it would be to pull on one of the strings and let the bikini fall free…

He swallowed in an effort to calm his raging hormones, then jogged to catch up with Shayna once she was under the shade of a tree. He snaked his arms around her waist, and she giggled. Turning her in his arms, he brought his mouth down on hers.

Her laugh turned into a moan of pleasure. He had startled her with the kiss, he knew, but he felt her body responding to his, growing hot against him. Slowly, she moved her fingers up his arms to his shoulders. Arched her breasts into his chest. It would be so easy to take her from this public spot to a place where there was some privacy and show her the depth of his desire for her.

But instead, he broke the kiss. Shayna's eyes were wide

as she stared up at him, her lips parted. She was the sexiest woman he'd ever laid eyes on.

"Yeah," he said slowly. "You are definitely a sex kitten." And he wanted to make her purr.

"A-are you ready to climb the falls?" she asked.

He was ready for far more than that, but he didn't say so. Instead, he ran the tip of his finger along her jawline and said, "I'm ready."

It was hard to pull apart from her, but Donovan did. He took her hand and walked with her to the base of the falls. There, he looked upward. People were climbing the rocks along the sides. It appeared that every ten feet or so there was a natural landing within the rocks, which housed shallow pools of water. About five people were in the first such shallow pool, smiling as someone took their photo.

"Would you like me to take your picture?" came the sound of a man's voice, rich with a Jamaican accent.

Donovan turned to see a smiling young man with a camera.

"You don't have to buy it if you don't like it," the man continued. "You can view the photos on your way out. If you like them, they are only ten dollars each."

"Definitely," Donovan said. He wanted a photo to mark the memory of this time with Shayna in this beautiful place.

The man positioned them at the base of the falls where he took a picture with the waterfall as a backdrop behind them. Donovan held Shayna close to him, posing with her as if she were his girlfriend or his lover.

The young man snapped a couple of shots with them, then lowered the camera. "Newlyweds, right?"

Shayna and Donovan exchanged glances. Shayna shrugged slightly, letting him know he could handle the situation as he saw fit.

"Actually, we're engaged," Donovan said. "We haven't set the date yet."

"Do it soon, mon," the man said. "I wouldn't let a foxy lady like her get away."

"Oh, you bet," Donovan told him.

The man also had them climb the first few rocks so that he could take a photo of them actually ascending the falls.

A group of about twenty people were climbing the falls ahead of Shayna and Donovan, each one holding hands to form a human chain. Shayna walked ahead of Donovan, but he was directly behind her. As she stumbled slightly on a slippery rock, Donovan quickly reached out and placed a hand on her hip to help steady her.

"Be careful, baby," Donovan said.

Baby. It was a slip of the tongue, Shayna was certain it had to have been. But it sounded so nice rolling off his lips.

They climbed a few more feet until they reached the first landing. Shayna waded into the shallow pool and perched herself on a large rock upon which the water was splashing. As the cold water cascaded over her body, she first gasped from the shock of the cool temperature, and then she began to giggle.

Donovan came beside her, and the waterfall splashed over him, as well. He pulled her onto his knee, secured his arms around her waist and nuzzled his nose in her neck.

She knew that his legs were muscular, but sitting on one of them now she could feel just how strong and powerful it was. A very big part of her wanted to stroke those thighs, tease him with her touch. She actually had to curl her fingers into her palms to make sure she didn't act on her desire.

She didn't see any of Donovan's family as they continued to climb up the falls, stopping at times in the areas where there were shallow pools and swimming a little. The falls were surrounded by trees and shrubs along its perimeter, adding to the absolute beauty of the place. Being here, Shayna felt certain that at least a portion of the Garden of Eden had looked like this.

After a good forty minutes of climbing, they found a fairly large pool of water near the top. They stopped there and swam for a little bit—and stole lots of kisses. It was hard not to be inspired by the romantic setting.

Moving to the center of this particular pool, beneath the spray of the waterfall, Shayna slipped her arms around Donovan's neck and also wrapped her legs around his waist. This pool of water was deep enough to hide most of their bodies, giving Shayna the courage to be a little more flirtatious.

"You're loving this, aren't you?" Donovan asked. "Loving that you're driving me crazy. And knowing that as much as I want to, this isn't the time nor place for me to touch you."

Shayna looked around. No one was immediately beside them. Some were already ascending the rocky stairs on the far side. Others were a good distance away.

Shayna grinned at him. "No one's looking at us."

Donovan's eyes widened. "What exactly do you want me to do?"

That was a loaded question. One Shayna could not answer in the way she wanted. Because what she wanted for him to do was something that would surely get them arrested if they tried to do it here.

"I just want to kiss you again," Shayna said.

And so he did, pressing his hot mouth down on hers, forcing his tongue between her parted lips. Her body exploded with heat. She opened her mouth to him, letting his tongue go deeper and sighing with the pleasure of it. It was a hot and desperate kiss, far too inappropriate for public, but Shayna didn't care. All she wanted right now was to indulge in this flirtation to the fullest. So she kissed Donovan wantonly, kissed him as though he was the man she was supposed to be with here on her honeymoon.

As he kissed her, his fingers skimmed the side of one of her breasts. Shayna mewled, wishing he could touch the part of her breast that craved his fingers but knowing he couldn't.

He moved with her through the water to the side, where he gently leaned Shayna's body against a large rock. Her legs were still wrapped around him, and as he kissed her senseless, he held her more tightly and she clung to him.

She could feel his arousal between them. Large and hard. Her body trembled from the force of her lust for him.

She had set out to tease him, but she had ended up torturing herself. Because her greatest desire right now was for Donovan to slip out of his swimming trunks and to pull off her bikini bottom and quench the thirst she had for him.

Donovan broke the kiss and moved his lips to her ear.

"This is killing me," he whispered, echoing her thoughts.

"It's killing me, too," Shayna admitted. She had her palms resting on Donovan's chest, and she could feel the beat of his heart beneath her fingers. It was racing.

"I want to make love to you," Donovan said, then gently nibbled on her earlobe.

Oh, Lord. That felt so good. A shiver of delight ran down her spine. "I want that, too."

"I'm almost willing to take a taxi back to the hotel and finish what we started. Because I don't know how much more of this I can take."

"I have money," Shayna blurted out. "I can pay for the taxi."

"So do I," Donovan said. "Do you want to do this? You want to leave?"

Shayna nodded. "Yes."

"I'll have to find my family. Let them know we're going."

"Then let's do it now," Shayna said. "Because I don't want to wait a moment longer to be with you."

Chapter 16

Shayna giggled into Donovan's shoulder as they sat in the backseat of the taxi.

"What's so funny?" Donovan asked.

"I'm thinking about what we told your brother," Shayna explained. While Shayna and Donovan had been in that uppermost pool of water creating their own steam, Antwon and Lynda had appeared with their children. Shayna had been so startled to see them, especially given that she had been wrapped around Donovan at the time.

"You don't think he believed us?"

Shayna erupted in a fit of giggles. "Not a chance."

Donovan had given his brother the lame excuse that Shayna hadn't been feeling very well. His brother's eyes had narrowed with suspicion while a smirk had played on his mouth. Donovan had gone on to say that Shayna had developed a headache and that they would be returning to the hotel by cab.

"Is that why you were giving her mouth-to-mouth?" Antwon had asked.

"No, seriously. She's got a headache," Donovan had insisted.

That had been their story, and they stuck to it as they said goodbye to other family members. But Shayna wasn't naive enough to believe that any of them believed they wanted to do anything other than get into bed.

"My brother probably won't give me the pictures of us until I tell him everything," Donovan said. He'd asked Antwon to look for and buy the photos the photographer had taken of them together at the base of the falls.

"And will you?" Shayna asked. "Tell him everything?"

Donovan leaned close and whispered in her ear, "Some things are meant only to be shared between two people."

Her entire body thrummed from the deep timbre of his voice.

At last the taxi arrived at the hotel, and Donovan paid the driver. He and Shayna all but jumped out of the car. The walk down that incredibly long hallway to her room seemed to take even longer today. But she and Donovan walked briskly, both of them unable to wait until they could be alone behind closed doors.

When they finally got to her room and she began to open the door, Donovan encircled her waist from behind with his hands, pulling her against him. He was hard and ready.

Shayna quickly threw open the door and rushed into the room. Donovan followed her and closed the door behind them. And then he bolted it.

Shayna locked eyes with his as he took a few brisk steps toward her. Then he was drawing her into his arms and pressing his hot mouth down on hers. Shayna moaned against his lips. Her entire body filled with heat as his tongue delved into her mouth. He slipped his hands into her hair, holding her steady as he kissed her until she was breathless.

Shayna pressed her hands against Donovan's strong pecs. She kneaded the flesh through his shirt, the feel of his hard muscles thrilling her. She wanted to feel him against her skin to skin, so she moved her hands lower to the hem of his shirt and slipped them beneath.

She skimmed the tips of her fingers over the hard grooves of his stomach muscles. Slowly, she moved them higher until she brushed his flat nipples.

Donovan growled. His own hands made their way down her back until he reached her butt. He squeezed and teased and pulled her closer, holding her against his erection.

His hands went lower still, to the hem of her dress. And then he was lifting it upward and pulling it over her head.

Shayna's body grew hotter when Donovan's eyes deliciously drank in the sight of her. It was the kind of look that made her want to strip out of her bikini and stand naked in front of him. Because his eyes alone set her body on fire.

Donovan kissed her again, and while he did he slipped his hands beneath the top bikini straps. Pulled them down. Shayna moaned in anticipation.

Donovan moved his hands to the swell of her breasts, where he teased the flesh with the tips of his fingers. Her bathing suit was loose but not exposing her breasts. Donovan continued to set her skin on fire with his light touch—so near to the part of her she was desperate for him to caress.

The bathing suit went lower, and at last his palms covered her nipples. Shayna sighed from the electrifying pleasure.

Donovan broke the kiss and flashed the sexiest of smiles at her before his eyes went lower to where his hands were.

"You're gorgeous," he whispered. And then he kissed her again, but his lips didn't stay at her mouth for long. They soon moved to the underside of her jaw, then trailed a path of heat down her neck and lower to the apex of her breasts. He twirled his thumbs over her nipples, making them erect and sending delicious tingles through her body.

When his thumb moved to the side of her left breast, Shayna held her breath. Because she knew what was coming next. And when Donovan's mouth closed over her nipple, the pleasure was so intense it felt like heaven.

Donovan worked his tongue and mouth over her breast until she was digging her fingers into his back and moaning. He moved his mouth from that breast to the other, skillfully covering her other nipple.

Had anything ever felt this good? There was something in the way Donovan touched her and used his tongue that set her body on fire in a way she had never experienced.

Donovan moved his mouth back to hers and kissed her deeply once more. He broke the kiss only to pull his own shirt over his head. Then he took Shayna's hands and led her to the bed.

She lay back, holding his gaze as she did. He was gorgeous. All those hard muscles and a beautiful face…he was a fantasy come to life.

And for now, he was hers.

"Do you have a condom?" Shayna asked. She didn't want to break the moment, but she was nothing if not practical. She wasn't on the Pill, so they would need to use protection.

"I picked some up this morning before we left," Donovan explained.

So he had been thinking along the same lines she had. Knowing that today was the day they would end up right here, in this exact position.

She kissed him again while running her palms up and down his arms. Then she kissed his neck, then his strong shoulder blade.

Donovan eased back and then reached for her bikini

bottoms. Shayna held her breath. After this, there was no turning back.

And she didn't want to turn back. She wanted to experience everything with her fantasy man.

His eyes locked with hers as he pulled the straps on one side of the bikini bottom loose. Then he pulled the other.

The bikini bottom gave way.

Shayna raised her hips, allowing Donovan to fully remove the bottom piece. A ragged breath escaped Donovan's lips as he pulled the last of her clothing away. She lay before him on the bed with her knees slightly bent, naked as the day she was born. It was completely thrilling to be naked before him like this, to see his eyes darken with lust and to know that she was the cause of that.

"You are a vision," Donovan said to Shayna. "Believe me when I tell you this—you're the most beautiful woman I've ever laid eyes on."

The words stoked the embers burning within her. "I want to see you, too," she said. "All of you."

"Then take it off," he told her, a twinkle in his eye.

Slowly, Shayna sat up. Donovan was standing at the edge of the bed, so she scooted over to him. She held his waist and pressed her mouth against his belly, giving him a slow, wet kiss outside of his belly button. Before she disrobed him, she lowered her hands to his thighs and gently dragged her nails along them, moving upward. Donovan's guttural groan was her reward.

She teased him with her fingers along his inner thighs. Lord, but those thighs were massive. Perfectly sculpted. She could not wait to feel them between her own.

She kissed his belly again while pulling his boxers down. And when he was naked, she eased back to look at him.

He was beautiful. His arousal was hard and large. He was ready for her as she was for him.

Gazing up at Donovan, she moved her hands up, as well, over his chest. In a flash, Donovan snagged her wrists. And then he was on top of her, kissing her with a raging hunger.

He was a great kisser. And he seemed to love doing it. Though they were naked and she wanted him inside of her, he was in no hurry.

And why hurry? They had all day.

But finally he eased off her and walked over to where he had placed his bag when they'd entered the room. He dug around until he found a condom.

Shayna shamelessly checked him out. His firm butt, those strong thighs from behind. A delicious wave of desire rocked her to her core.

When he faced her again, the condom was on. He moved toward her stealthily, like a jaguar moving in on its prey. He eased over her on the bed once more, keeping his upper body elevated with the strength of those ripped arms.

He nibbled the flesh of her bottom lip as his hand moved between them, to her center. "Oh, baby," Donovan rasped, his fingers playing over her. "You're ready for me."

"Yes," Shayna said, her voice fluttering.

Donovan kissed her again, urging his own tongue into her mouth at the same time he entered her with a slow, careful thrust. Shayna gasped, the pleasure more intense and gratifying than anything she had ever known.

They moved slowly together at first, finding their rhythm. And then the pace increased, their movements getting faster along with their breathing. All the while he kissed her, making what they were sharing far more intimate than the simple act of having sex.

He filled her completely, each stroke taking her to a place of bliss so breathtaking that she never wanted to come back to earth. Being in Donovan's arms, she felt whole in a way she never had felt before.

Donovan stroked her nipple, increasing the delicious sensations assailing her body. She locked her legs around his waist, secured her arms around his chest and held on for the ride.

And soon, the sensations were building in her like a rising tide about to crash to the shore. Moments later, every nerve ending in her body became electrified as an earth-shattering release claimed her.

She clung to Donovan and cried out his name, wave after delicious wave washing over her.

"Yes, baby," Donovan said into her ear a moment later. "That's it, sweetheart."

Donovan slowed his pace and kissed her cheek softly. "Look at me, baby," he said.

She opened her eyes and stared into the face of the man she had just given herself to completely. He grinned down at her before capturing her lips in a slow and passionate kiss.

She moved her hips against Donovan, urging him to go faster, wanting him to feel the same exquisite bliss she had just felt. He moved faster, and within seconds, she felt the crescendo rising deep within her once more. She arched her back, moaning as she was losing herself once again to the luscious sensations.

And when Donovan drove into her with a deep, hard thrust, Shayna went over the edge with him, both of them crying out each other's name.

Their bodies spent, they lay together breathing heavily but not moving. A sheen of sweat covered both of their skin.

Donovan ran the tip of his tongue along the side of her jaw, and when he got near her mouth he brushed his lips against hers. Shayna placed a palm on his cheek and stared into his eyes.

"What?" Donovan asked.

"I'm just thinking—"

"Thinking what?"

She stroked his face. "That I have never felt this amazing. Ever."

"Neither have I, sweetheart."

What was happening between them? Not just the explosiveness of their lovemaking, but everything that had led up to it. Because as much as Shayna had led herself to believe that this would be a casual affair, she knew now that it wasn't. That on some level, her emotions had gotten involved.

"And I'm not through with you yet," Donovan said.

"Oh?"

"Not a chance." Donovan tweaked her nipple, and just like that she was aroused again. He kissed a path from her neck down her torso, stopping only when he'd reached her belly button. Still stroking her nipple, he dipped his tongue into the groove of her belly button, licking it slowly.

He brought his hand lower, skimming his fingers over her hips and then along her inner thigh. Shayna held her breath as his fingers moved over her center.

He stroked her, and she gasped. One stroke, but it had been like she'd been touched with a live wire. And when he kissed her inner thigh, Shayna gripped the bedspread with both hands.

"I want to please you this way," Donovan said.

In reply, Shayna arched her back and closed her eyes. She wanted that, too.

He moved his mouth higher along her inner thigh, closer now to the portal of her pleasure. And when his tongue touched her there, a long, hot breath oozed out of her. Soon, she was on the edge of that cliff again, about to fall over.

And when she did fall, crying out his name, all she could think was that this first, sweet taste of Donovan was not going to be enough.

Not hardly.

* * *

Donovan couldn't get enough of her. Every sigh, every moan, turned him on in a way he had never imagined possible.

Donovan would never tire of the feel of her soft, warm body in his arms, the feel of her soft lips against his own. And the way she responded to him stoked his hunger all the more.

They stayed in her room and made love for the entire afternoon, trying out different positions and learning with each passing minute more of what the other liked. Close to five o'clock, with Shayna in his arms, they drifted off to sleep.

It was after six o'clock when Donovan's eyes popped open. Shayna was still in his arms, her chest rising and falling with each steady breath. She felt comfortable in his arms, as though she was meant to be there. And Donovan knew that he wanted her in his life always. Fate had brought them together, and he didn't want to let her go.

Shayna stirred. He stroked her arm, and she turned to look at him.

"Hey," she said softly.

"Hey, yourself."

"What time is it?"

"Nine minutes after six."

Shayna circled her arm around his neck, telling him with that simple motion that she wasn't nearly finished with him yet either.

"I'm supposed to leave tomorrow," Donovan said.

"Tomorrow?" Shayna's eyes widened in alarm.

Donovan nodded. "Yeah. It was a five-day trip."

"No," Shayna protested softly. "Please tell me you're not serious."

"Do you want me to stay?"

"Would you?"

"Yeah," Donovan said with no hesitation. "I would. When do you leave?"

"My flight is Sunday afternoon."

"So we could have four more days together." Donovan didn't care the cost. He wanted to stay with this woman who had so enthralled him. After having a taste of her, the last thing he could do was say goodbye in the morning.

Donovan eased up on an elbow. "Do you want me to stay with you?"

"I'm not ready for this to end," Shayna admitted.

Donovan wondered if she was feeling what he was feeling. The connection was beyond the physical. Yes, they were physically drawn to each other. That was obvious and natural. But Donovan's desire to stay with her went beyond simply the physical need he had for her.

"I'll go to the front desk," Donovan explained. "You've got this room to yourself, so I see no reason why I shouldn't be able to stay with you. I'll have to pay more for the all-inclusive portion, of course, but that's okay."

Shayna sat up beside Donovan. "I should go with you. If this works out, they're going to need my approval to have you join me in my room."

Donovan slipped his fingers into her hair and drew her face to his. He kissed her, reigniting his own burning desire for her as well as her own.

He lay on his back, pulling her onto him as he did. Shayna straddled her legs over his body. He was hard again and needing her desperately.

She pressed her breasts against his chest and kissed him back with wanton abandon. He caressed her back, her hips. And then with a groan, he broke the kiss.

He wanted nothing more than to enter her, make them one again. But he needed to do so with a condom.

"Condom," he said.

He had placed the box of condoms on the dresser so they would be more readily accessible. Shayna eased off his body and reached for the box. As she did, Donovan's eyes drank in the sight of her naked form. She was gorgeous—and not just on the outside. It was easy to tell that she was a beautiful person on the inside, as well.

How had he gotten so lucky to meet this woman?

He didn't know. All he knew was that he didn't want to let her go.

She sat beside him, opening the condom wrapper and then putting it on him. The moment she was done, Donovan moved her onto him again and they picked up right where they had left off.

He thrust inside of her, the feeling of pleasure beyond anything that he could put into words. And when they had both ridden a wave and come crashing onto the shore, Donovan knew that he would pay any price to stay with her for four more days.

But what he hoped was that after this trip was over, they would have far more than this time on the island together.

Chapter 17

Donovan was able to rearrange his flight and hotel stay so that he could remain on the island with Shayna until Sunday. His flight would be at ten, meaning he had to leave by seven o'clock on Sunday morning.

He spent Wednesday night with her, and on Thursday he moved his things to her room. And from that point on they were like a true couple—inseparable. They spent much of their time in the bedroom, but also a lot of time outdoors, strolling hand in hand, swimming in the sea and doing a few more excursions.

Aside from Dunn's River Falls, the sunset cruise on Saturday evening was Shayna's favorite excursion with Donovan. But it was also the most bittersweet.

It was where they were now, sitting together on the back of a catamaran, holding hands and staring out at the orange-colored sky.

This was the last day Shayna had with him. The week had been incredible, and she'd ended up meeting someone who had been exactly what she needed. But their time together was coming to an end.

The realization made her sad. If she could extend this trip with Donovan another week, she would. She did not want to head back home—and back to reality.

"What are you thinking?" Donovan asked.

Shayna snuggled against his side, not wanting to voice her thoughts. She simply wanted to enjoy the last night they had together here.

"Are you sad?"

"It's just…this has been such an amazing week. Far more than I ever expected."

"And you hate for it to end," Donovan supplied.

Shayna nodded.

Donovan was silent as he stared out at the sunset, and Shayna did the same. But after a moment he asked her, "Who says this has to end?"

Shayna didn't speak—just met Donovan's eyes. There were others on the boat, as well, but suddenly it seemed like just the two of them were there.

What he was saying was a nice fantasy. She couldn't deny that. But was it reality?

"I want you to know," Donovan went on, his voice low, "that you're the first person I've made love to since…since Nina. That isn't something I take lightly."

Shayna had suspected that based on what he'd said about not having dated, but she hadn't been sure. He could have had a casual affair or two. Other men in his situation would have. She wasn't quite sure what to make of the admission.

When Shayna didn't speak, Donovan continued. "Something special is happening between us, Shayna. I want to keep seeing you when we get back home."

"You do?" Shayna's heart began to pound wildly.

"Yes. And I'm hoping you want the same thing."

Shayna looked away, off into the distance. The sun had dipped even lower, and the sky was now a mix of dark purple and orange. She wanted to say yes—that she did want to keep seeing Donovan, as well. But they lived in two different cities. In two different states. How realistic was it that they were going to be able to keep alive what they had started here?

"I—" Shayna began, then abruptly stopped.

Donovan placed a finger beneath her chin and gently turned her face so that she could look at him. "You what?"

"I don't know," Shayna said softly.

"What don't you know?"

"It's a nice idea, but—"

"Why does there have to be a but? We've connected, Shayna. You can't deny that."

"We've connected in this magical place," Shayna said, gesturing with her arm toward the sea. "But this isn't the real world, Donovan. In the real world you have your life and I have mine. And I'm not saying that I don't want to continue a relationship, but I also don't want to be unrealistic."

And what she really didn't want was to suffer a second broken heart. Because what she had experienced with Donovan had been so intense and wonderful that she knew it would be easy for her feelings to deepen for him. And if she let herself believe that a future could develop from this, she'd go home with expectations. And if those expectations didn't pan out, she would be devastated.

"Do you believe in fate?" Donovan asked.

Did she? She wrote about it, that was for sure. And she wanted to believe it. But her experience with Vince had shown her that just because a person wanted to believe something didn't make it real.

"I believe that everyone has good intentions. I believe that you mean it when you say you want to continue a relationship with me. But I also know that this has been only a week. A wonderful week, granted, but still just a week. I was in a place in my life where I needed something positive, and maybe you, too. We both came together at a time when we needed each other…but is it more than that?"

Even as she asked the question, Shayna's stomach fluttered with an uneasy sensation. Her brain and heart were not in sync.

"I think it is, yeah. I think we met each other for a reason. And it wasn't just because you needed someone and I needed someone at this particular juncture in our lives."

Shayna said nothing. She didn't want to allow herself to get hopeful. She would not be able to deal with the heartbreak if things didn't work out.

"Look at me, Shayna." She did. And then Donovan said, "I've fallen in love with you."

"What?" Shayna asked breathlessly.

"It's true. I felt it almost from the beginning."

The words had set her pulse racing, but she felt a mix of excitement and profound fear. How could he know that he loved her already?

"Oh, Donovan." Shayna sighed.

He fiddled with a lock of her hair and stared deeply into her eyes. "I mean it, Shayna."

"Maybe you do. But a few days in Jamaica—is that really long enough to fall in love with someone?"

"Is there a required time that you need to know someone before you know you're in love with them?" Donovan asked.

Shayna didn't answer the question. Every rational part of her mind was telling her that no, a short time in Jamaica was not long enough. Her heart, however, wanted to believe something else.

"I don't doubt that you're sincere about staying in touch when we get back to the States. But…"

"But what?"

"You know how you meet people on vacation, and during that time you're as thick as thieves? You promise to stay in touch when you get back home. To call or e-mail. But you never do."

"You don't think we will?" Donovan asked.

Shayna gave him a skeptical look. A few beats passed before she spoke. "This time with you has been nice. We've been good company for each other. In truth, you've been better company for me because I came here alone. But... Look, it happened to a friend of mine. She went on vacation and met this guy she was crazy about. During their one week in Hawaii, she fell hard for him. Apparently he fell as hard for her. They both returned home and started a long-distance relationship. Within two months, it was over."

"That won't happen for us," Donovan said.

"How can you be so sure?"

"Because of how I feel right now." Donovan trailed a hand down her arm.

Shayna's stomach clenched. She wanted to believe what Donovan was saying, but she also knew that no matter how well meaning he might be, things would change once they got back home.

Shayna stood and wandered to the side of the boat. She looked at the shore, which they were now approaching.

Donovan came to stand behind her, placing a hand on her hip. And Shayna knew this was going to be a hard goodbye. Perhaps it would be impossible to say goodbye to the fantasy.

She turned and faced Donovan. "I really am happy that I met you. I'll never forget this time we shared."

"Are you trying to give me the brush-off?" Donovan asked. There was a smile in his eyes as he asked the question, and Shayna realized that at all times, he had a positive demeanor.

Even in the face of losing someone he'd loved, he was still a glass-is-half-full kind of person.

"I'm not giving you the brush-off. But I want to be realistic. In a way that my friend who went to Hawaii—"

Donovan placed a finger on Shayna's lips, silencing her. Then he slowly moved his face close to hers. First he kissed one cheek, then the other. Then her forehead. A slow and lazy kiss that had sweet sensations tingling along her skin.

"You want to know what I think of your theory about people on vacation?" he asked, moving his lips close to hers but keeping them about an inch away.

Shayna could feel the heat of his breath on her skin. She could feel the heat within her growing to a fever pitch. Suddenly, she wasn't thinking about tomorrow or whether or not they'd be in touch again. All she was thinking about was right here, right now. About how amazingly alive she felt when Donovan touched her. Heck, his eyes alone set her skin on fire every time he looked at her.

"I don't buy it," Donovan told her. "Not for a second."

With the way he had just kissed her, Shayna didn't want to buy it either. "I don't want to get hurt again," she said softly.

"I don't want to get hurt again. No one does."

"I'd love to believe that we could have a future, but seven days, six really—"

"Isn't long enough to fall in love with someone," Donovan stated, reiterating her earlier point of view. He sighed. "What if you're wrong?"

The boat came to shore, and people began to line up so they could exit. Shayna followed those people, not wanting to have to answer Donovan's question.

What if she *was* wrong? She could deal with that. But what she couldn't deal with was being right. Being right would mean more pain, and she didn't know if her heart could deal with that.

Shayna held her sandals in her hand as they exited the boat. Donovan was beside her, but he was silent.

"Why don't we stay in touch for a couple of months?" Shayna suggested. "If we feel the same way at that time—"

"I will."

"Then we won't have lost anything," Shayna said.

"We will have lost two months. And from personal experience, I know that you don't always have the amount of time you think you do."

This was too much for Shayna to deal with. She remembered how heartbroken her friend had been after her Hawaii romance had failed to thrive after a couple of months. Realism and fantasy fought for control of her brain and heart.

As she and Donovan walked together across the sand, Shayna suddenly turned to him and said, "I think I need some time alone. You can go back to the room, and I'll take a walk."

The disappointment on Donovan's face was clear. But he nodded nonetheless. Then he said, "Actually, I'll take the walk. You should go back to the room. After what happened with Garth, it's probably not the best thing for you to be out at night walking around alone."

She nodded. "Okay."

She continued walking beside him, but he didn't take her hand. The emotional distance between them had grown, and she took full responsibility for that. It was just that suddenly she was unable to let herself get lost in the fantasy as she had earlier in the week.

Because to do so would only be prolonging the inevitable.

That inevitable was that he would go on with his life, and she would go on with hers. The knowledge hurt her more than she'd ever expected it would.

Donovan walked with her until they got to their building.

Shayna looked at him and said, "I'll be fine getting upstairs on my own."

"I'll walk you up, just in case."

He was a true gentleman. Far more than most men these days. "Okay."

At the room door, Donovan spoke. "How much time do you need?"

"I'm not sure. Enough to think, I guess."

"All right."

Shayna went into the room, and Donovan began to stroll back down the hallway. She felt awful—as if they'd just broken up.

He'd changed his plane ticket to be around a few extra days with her. And those days had been the most fabulous of her thirty-two years. Right now, they should be making love again. Making the most of the time they had left together.

Whirling around, Shayna ran back to the door. She threw it open and looked for Donovan, ready to tell him that she didn't want time alone after all. That she wanted him. One last time. In her bed. To make love to her so wildly she would never forget him.

But she didn't see him.

"Donovan," Shayna called. She listened. Heard nothing.

"Donovan!" she called louder.

Again, nothing.

She went back into the room and hurried onto the balcony, where she scanned the area below for any sign of Donovan. He was nowhere.

Shayna went back into the room and lay on the bed. After a few minutes of feeling disappointed, she told herself that maybe it was best this way.

Best that she lie here alone and begin the process of coming down from fantasyland and back to reality.

Chapter 18

Hours later, shortly after one in the morning, Shayna heard the soft rapping on her door. Knowing it had to be Donovan, her heart went into overdrive.

But why was he knocking? He had a key. She had expected him to simply come back into the room after giving her some time.

When the knocking sounded again, she climbed off the bed and went to the door.

Her hands were jittery as she reached for the knob. Why was she so nervous to see him?

Because the fantasy had come to an end. In six hours, he would be leaving for home. She was leaving five hours later. He would return to Maryland and she to Buffalo. That would be that.

It was the way these vacation relationships worked. She had already accepted that.

But when she opened the door and saw Donovan, she felt a hot rush of attraction at the mere sight of him standing with his shoulder resting against her door frame, which told her that her feelings for him were anything but over. He still excited her. Her body still reacted to him.

"Why didn't you open the door?" Shayna asked. Surely he didn't feel unwelcome because of what she'd said to him.

"I couldn't find my key."

"Oh."

He stared at her and she at him. And with that one look, heat ignited between them.

Donovan didn't say anything, just moved into the room with the stealth of a jaguar, his eyes locked on hers. Shayna swallowed a breath and took two steps backward. Not because she was afraid but because she wanted to allow enough room for him to close the door.

And that's just what Donovan did the moment he'd crossed the threshold. His gaze still holding hers, he pushed the door closed behind him. And with his next move, he wrapped an arm around Shayna's waist.

She gasped as he pulled her against his strong chest, her soft breasts pressing against his hard muscles. Her lips parted, and his mouth captured hers.

There was nothing gentle about the kiss. It was hungry and hot, their tongues tangling almost desperately. Shayna closed her eyes, surrendering completely to Donovan.

As he kissed her, his hands framed her face. He stroked each cheek in unison. Then both undersides of her jaw. Then both sides of her neck, moving steadily lower until his hands came together at the apex of her breasts.

Shayna moaned into his mouth, his touch exciting her as much as it had the first time. More, perhaps. Because now she knew what to expect. Knew the gentle exquisiteness with which Donovan could please her.

She wanted his hands on her breasts. His mouth. Taking her back to those unimaginable heights of pleasure.

Donovan stepped forward, forcing Shayna backward, until finally her legs collided with the bed. She went down, Donovan going down with her, his lips still fused with hers.

She gripped his shoulders and parted her legs, the clothes between their bodies only adding to the pleasure. Teasing her with thoughts of what was to come.

Donovan settled between her thighs, and every last protest fled Shayna's mind. She didn't think about goodbye or what would happen in the next hour, let alone tomorrow. Because more than anything, she wanted to be right where she was, in Donovan's arms.

One of his hands slipped beneath her camisole, and the feel of his skin against her skin... How was it that he made her body come alive in a way she had never known before?

As his hand inched upward, his mouth moved from hers, trailing hot kisses along the underside of her jaw. His mouth went lower. His hand went higher. And when his fingers skimmed the fullness of her breast, a shuddery breath escaped her.

Shayna arched her back as his fingers reached higher. And when they found her erect nipple, she sighed in pure pleasure. He played with the tight bud, stroking it gently, then kneading it, until Shayna's breaths came in quick, sharp bursts.

Then Donovan was pushing her camisole up and bringing his mouth down. Shayna's center throbbed with exquisite pleasure as his tongue flicked over her hardened peak.

He worked magic with his mouth and tongue, each delicious stroke taking her closer and closer to the edge of bliss. The man was strong, yet gentle, and he knew just how to touch her.

In his arms, she felt a sense of completion she'd never known.

While his mouth and tongue pleased her breasts, he placed a hand on her knee. He made a lazy circle with the tip of his finger along her skin, much the same way his tongue was doing to her nipple. She was powerless to resist him. She would stay here another week with him if that's what he asked her to do right now.

His hand slipped beneath her skirt and trailed along her inner thigh. When his fingers stroked her center, Shayna knew that if this was the last thing she ever experienced, she could die a happy woman.

"You're so beautiful," Donovan murmured. He kissed a path down her torso. "I wish we could stay here forever like this, forgetting the entire world." He kissed her navel. "With me pleasing you endlessly."

Shayna held her breath as his lips went lower. And when his mouth came down on her center, she gasped, her body quivering.

He took her over the edge with his tongue. She thrashed her head and cried out his name, her body filling not just with pleasure but with a feeling of complete connection to another person.

Donovan kissed her inner thigh, then stood and quickly undid his khaki shorts. Before he slipped them off, he reached onto the night table and got a condom from the box.

Shayna's body was still trembling as she watched him slip out of his shorts and white briefs, revealing his large arousal. Seeing the evidence of his desire for her made a hot flush sweep over her body. Donovan put the condom on, then stepped toward her. Shayna's eyes fluttered shut as he settled between her thighs.

And in the next glorious moment, he filled her, completing her. With each stroke, he reached a place deep inside of her, far deeper than the mere physical pleasure.

It reached to her soul.

Because that was what making love with Donovan was. The connecting of her soul with his.

He increased his pace, moving faster, reaching deeper. Shayna wrapped her legs around his waist, holding on tight, enjoying the exquisite ride. With her fists, she gripped the bedspread.

His breathing was coming faster. So was hers. Together, they had fallen into that easy rhythm. Their bodies responding to each other as if they had been doing this for years. Giving and receiving the ultimate pleasure.

"Oh, Donovan…" She was on the edge again, about to topple over into that most special of places. She wanted him to go there with her.

She tightened her legs even more, working her hips in time to his movements. All the while she flicked her tongue over his collarbone, tasting the hint of salt on his skin.

"Baby," Donovan groaned. "Oh, sweetheart.…"

And she knew he was on the edge with her. She worked her hips faster, dug her teeth into his flesh.

She moaned, he groaned, and then they were both lost. Lost in each other. Over the edge at the same time, sharing the same exquisite sensations as one.

Afterward, they lay together, going still. Neither one seemed to want to move. Shayna knew that she could stay like this with Donovan and be content for hours. To fall asleep like this and know that she would wake up with Donovan in her arms.

In her bed.

In her life.

A moan of sadness clawed at her throat, unexpected. She tried to stifle it.

"Hey," Donovan said. He eased back to look at her, staring at her with that look of genuine concern that was her undoing.

Why was she feeling so emotional? She'd wanted this. Wanted one last goodbye. She would stay in touch with him when they got back home, but she held no illusions that they would realistically pick up where they left off. She'd known that when she'd started the affair. She had known that before he came back to her door.

So what was her problem?

Donovan kissed her cheek. "What is it?"

"I guess I don't want to say goodbye," she admitted sadly.

"It's not goodbye," he told her. "It's see you later."

She frowned. She wanted to believe that. But was it possible? She didn't want to get her hopes up only to get hurt again.

Because she knew that time, distance and perspective might change how they were both feeling.

But the truth was, with the way she felt now, she didn't expect her feelings to change. And yet it seemed impossible that she could have come to care for him so strongly in such a short time.

"I'd rather we just…"

"Just what?" Donovan asked.

Shayna didn't meet his eyes. It was too hard to look at him and say what she knew she had to say. "Just…not have any expectations. It'll be easier that way."

"I do have expectations, Shayna. Because I love you."

Shayna sighed. "I hear what you're saying, and I…I know you think you mean it. But six days…" Shayna paused a beat. "Rationally, we both know that isn't long enough to fall in love with someone."

Donovan didn't say anything. Instead, he put his finger beneath Shayna's chin and urged her face upward. Her face moved, but she kept her eyes averted.

"Look at me," Donovan said softly.

Another beat passed, then Shayna met his eyes.

"It wasn't just six days," Donovan said. "It was six nights."

Shayna's face flamed. An image of how they'd spent the last four of those nights flashed into her head. Their bodies slick with sweat, his tongue on her skin, her crying out his name.

"What are you thinking?" Donovan asked, but surely he had to know. Shayna was certain that it was written on her face.

"That…" she began, then paused. She summoned her courage. "I'm thinking that you're confusing lust with love."

"I'm not."

"Six days—and six nights—isn't long enough to know that you're in love with someone." She had to keep reminding herself of that before she got caught up in unrealistic expectations. That would be her downfall.

"And what if I told you that I fell in love with you that first day? The very first time I laid eyes on you."

Shayna searched Donovan's eyes. Searched to see if he was playing a game with her. But all she saw was tenderness and truth.

It touched her soul.

"I want to believe that," she said, her voice a whisper.

"But you've made up your mind, decided it can't be true—and you're not willing to be wrong."

Donovan's words struck a chord. In a big way. He had summed up Shayna's personality in one sentence. When she made a decision about something, that was it.

In the past, it had been easy.

But now…

"So you write romances, but you don't really believe it," Donovan said. A statement, not a question.

Shayna opened her mouth to protest, but what could she say? He was right. Even if she couldn't admit it. She'd written novel after novel where love was magical and unexpected and triumphed against all odds.

But those are just unrealistic fantasies, she thought, voicing one of the popular anti–romance novel views.

"I... I didn't say that. But—"

"But you don't believe it."

"I'm willing to stay in touch," Shayna said. "We stay in touch when we leave the island. If in two months, we still feel what we're feeling now, then great. And if not...neither one of us has to feel disappointed."

Sighing, Donovan eased his body off hers. "So what do we do now? Exchange phone numbers and e-mail addresses?"

He sounded upset.

"Well...yes."

"Am I allowed to call you? Or would you prefer to wait two months with no contact?"

"Donovan, I'm throwing you an olive branch."

"You think I want an olive branch?" he asked, baffled.

"I didn't—"

"If you want nothing more to do with me, just come out and tell me."

"That's not true," Shayna said. "But I need time. And I don't think that's unreasonable."

Donovan got off the bed, and Shayna thought he was going to leave the room. Instead, he went to his suitcase and withdrew an envelope.

"I've got the pictures from Dunn's River Falls," he said. "Why don't you pick one you like...if you want a reminder of us at all."

Shayna felt like crying. He was acting like she was dismissing him and their time together, when that wasn't the case at all. She simply wanted to guard her heart.

"I...I like the one with us at the base of the falls," she said after a moment. It was a beautiful shot. They looked like they were a couple in love.

"I like that one, too."

"I've got a scanner," Shayna said. "I can make a copy. I can make copies of both of them, actually."

Donovan nodded. "Do you promise if I give you both of these you'll send me copies?"

"Yes."

"Because unlike you, I'm not ready to forget what we shared here. Ever."

Chapter 19

There was no more making love that night.

In fact, there was a definite distance between them, a divide Shayna wasn't sure they'd ever overcome.

Donovan slept on one side of the bed, and she slept on the other. When he got up to get his things ready to leave, she pretended to still be asleep.

But she was awake, her heart aching.

Before Donovan left for the airport, he sat on the bed beside her and stroked her thigh. She opened her eyes then, pretending that she'd just woken.

"I'm leaving now, Shayna," Donovan had told her. "Please, know that everything I told you was true."

Then he kissed her softly on the lips, and Shayna somehow refrained from snaking her arms around his neck and pulling him close. Instead, she let him leave with the promise that they would be in touch.

Once he'd walked through the door, the tears came. She cried herself to sleep, wishing that things between her and

Donovan could be different but knowing that it was far too foolish to believe that they could be.

Shayna arrived home late that Sunday night, so she didn't call any of her family members. She sent Brianne a text message while at Pearson International Airport to let her know that she had landed safely and was okay and asked her to relay that message to her parents.

Monday morning, before Shayna could call her family to let them know that she had made it the rest of the way home safely, there was a knock on her door.

Shayna got out of bed, slipped into a robe, then made her way through her apartment and peered through the door's peephole.

Her sister stood there.

She opened the door, saying, "Brianne, what are you doing here?"

"I had to come see you," she said simply, moving into the apartment.

Shayna glanced at the clock. It was 9:26 a.m. "Right *now?*"

"I'm on my way to work," Brianne explained. "But I wanted to see you first."

"Why?" Shayna asked, eyeing Brianne with a guarded expression.

"Because I wanted to hear all about Jamaica." She sat on the sofa. "So, how was it?"

Shayna had the odd feeling that there was more to her sister's visit, but she simply said, "Jamaica was beautiful. And very relaxing. I had a great time."

"How good a time?" Brianne asked, her eyes narrowing with suspicion.

"What do you mean?"

"Oh, you know exactly what I mean."

Had Brianne taken one look at Shayna and realized there was something she wasn't telling her? Or was she just fishing?

"I had a very good time," Shayna replied simply. "And guess what—I'm over Vince. Completely."

"And did you have any *help* getting over Vince?" Brianne asked, raising an eyebrow.

Shayna and Brianne were pretty much in tune with what the other was thinking much of the time, but Shayna had never known her sister to be psychic. And yet she was asking the kind of questions that led Shayna to believe she *knew* something. But how could that be possible?

"I…I had the idyllic setting to help. And lots of books to occupy my mind."

Brianne planted her hands on her hips and scowled at Shayna. "Sis, if you don't tell me the real story…"

"I'm confused." She fiddled with the tie on her robe, not meeting Brianne's curious gaze. "Why do you think there's something I'm not telling you?"

"Oh, my goodness." Shayna looked at her sister in time to see her eyes light up. Brianne jumped to her feet and hurried over to Shayna. "Shay, you didn't. You *didn't,* right?"

"Didn't what?"

"Meet someone on your honeymoon!"

Shayna made a face as she stared at Brianne, truly not understanding how she could have any inkling as to what had transpired the past week when Shayna hadn't yet had a conversation with her.

"That look on your face! Oh, my God. You *did!* On your honeymoon!"

"First of all, Bree, please don't say I was on my *honeymoon.* I was on a…a vacation."

"Vacation? I thought you were going to heal."

"Okay, let's call it a rejuvenation trip. I needed to nurse my soul…and I did."

"Wow." Brianne looked at Shayna in awe. "You had an affair?"

"I don't understand where any of this is coming from," Shayna said, not wanting to spill the beans yet.

"I had a dream," Brianne admitted. "Two nights ago. A dream that you'd met someone. And it was so vivid that when I woke up, I had the feeling it was true."

"Why do you seem so excited? I thought you warned me not to get involved with anyone before I left."

"I know," Brianne said. "But then I watched *How Stella Got Her Groove Back* when you were gone, and it made me think that an affair might be just what you need."

"It wasn't an affair," Shayna said. "It was a fling."

"Oh, my goodness!" Brianne squealed and grabbed her sister's hands, squeezing the life out of them. "You got your groove back like Stella? Was he young? Did he have a cute Jamaican accent? Did he look like Taye Diggs?"

Shayna had to laugh at her sister's excitement. "No, he's not young. Well, he's two years younger than I am, but big deal. And no, he didn't have a Jamaican accent. He's from Maryland. And I think he's cuter than Taye Diggs."

Brianne squealed again, then clamped a hand down on her mouth.

"You just woke the last of my sleeping neighbors," Shayna said wryly.

"I know. I'm sorry. I'm just so…*shocked*. I can't believe you had a fling with someone!"

"You're not that shocked. You came here before work because you expected me to tell you exactly that."

"It's just that my dream seemed so real. Like a premonition. I can't believe I was right."

"He's really nice," Shayna said. "A total gentleman, very

charming, and it was easy to let down my walls and go for it. And he was just what I needed. Absolutely gorgeous on top of being so nice. A guy who was totally into me, one who couldn't understand how Vince could have betrayed me the night before our wedding. In a way, he became a substitute husband. We hung out together almost right from the start. And my God, we went to Dunn's River Falls, which has to be the most romantic place on earth. That's when I knew we would make love."

"Whoa," Brianne said, holding up both hands to form a T, the universal signal for "time out." "Make love?"

"You know what I mean."

Brianne eyed her skeptically. "You're talking about him like he was more than a fling. Almost like you made a love connection."

Was she? "No, of course not. It's just…he helped me not to be lonely."

Brianne raised her eyebrows.

"He was what I needed during a difficult time."

"And now what?"

"Now nothing."

"Have you been in touch with him since you've gotten back?"

Shayna's stomach fluttered. "I got a text from him while I was at the airport, yes. He let me know he'd gotten home safely."

"So you're staying in touch?"

"Yes." She shrugged, trying to be nonchalant. "I guess we will."

"You like him, don't you?" Brianne asked.

"Of course I like him. I wouldn't have slept with him otherwise."

"That's not what I mean. You *like* him."

"He's a really nice guy. I hope we can be friends for a long time."

"Friends?" Brianne said, doubtfully.

"Why not?" Shayna asked. "Obviously—"

"Obviously, the man is more than a fling. Casual hookups on vacation don't end with people gushing about the other person afterward. Talking about being friends. Usually people just move on happy that they had an itch scratched."

"And you would know because you've had *how* many vacation hookups?" Shayna said sarcastically. She was suddenly snippy because all this talk about Donovan was making her miss him, when what she wanted to do was find a way to put him out of her mind.

"Hey," Brianne said. "I'm not trying to say there's something wrong with being his friend. That's actually kind of special. But the fact that you spent all this time with him? Maybe—just maybe—your feelings are a little deeper than you are letting on. More than what I would expect for someone who was just a fling. You're forgetting I've been your sister for twenty-eight years. I know how to read you."

Shayna's heart began to beat a little faster. She couldn't entirely deny what her sister was saying. She did like Donovan. Something that all her sister's questions were making more evident to her.

No, in her heart of hearts she knew she could never categorize Donovan as simply a fling. He had been much more than that.

But still, for her own peace of mind, she had to find a way to close the door on the memory of the fabulous week they had shared.

Because she didn't want to end up devastated—the way her friend Cheryl had been after her island romance had crashed and burned once returning to the real world.

* * *

After her sister left, Shayna dutifully scanned the photos of her and Donovan at Dunn's River Falls and e-mailed them to him. Though she didn't want to, she kept checking her e-mail often for a reply from him during the day. About six hours later the reply came, a simple "Thanks. Take care."

Shayna frowned at the response, a profound sense of disappointment making her stomach clench. And yet what right did she have to feel disappointed? She was the one who'd told Donovan that it made sense to limit their communication for at least two months.

The rest of the week passed with no more e-mails or text messages from Donovan. And despite everything Shayna had said to Donovan about cooling things down, it bothered her. Even as she told herself that this was exactly the way she wanted things.

Several times, she contemplated sending him a message, a few lines to let him know she was thinking about him. But she didn't bother.

What was the point?

This initial phase of thinking about him every day, several times a day, would surely pass. She spent a lot of time retrieving the boxes Vince had delivered to her parents' house and unpacking those belongings, which helped occupy her thoughts. She'd spoken with her landlord, and at least she was going to be able to keep her apartment.

She also tried to get back into the routine of her regular life, which meant plotting a new novel to submit to her editor.

But nothing exciting came to her. At least not with a historical premise. In fact, she was suddenly thinking about a contemporary, perhaps featuring a man who was a successful business owner on top of the world—until he unexpectedly lost his fiancée.

"This is ridiculous," Shayna told herself the next Monday

afternoon when she realized the character she was creating was Donovan. When was she going to forget the man?

She got up and went to the kitchen, where she set about making a sandwich for lunch. She was putting the package of turkey slices back in the fridge when there was a knock on her door.

She was expecting a package from her publisher with copies of her newest book, which she would sign on Saturday at a bookstore in the Boulevard Mall in Amherst.

But instead of seeing a deliveryman, she opened the door to Vince.

She didn't speak for several seconds, beyond stunned.

"Hey," Vince said softly, the first to break the silence.

"What—what are you doing here?"

Vince didn't answer, just stepped into the apartment without being invited. Only when he was safely behind the apartment door did he venture to answer her.

"Shayna, I had to see you."

Shayna's heart pounded in her chest but not from a sense of elation. Rather, she felt a sense of dread. "Why?"

"Because I want to apologize," Vince said.

"You already did," Shayna pointed out. "There's no further need."

"Yes, Shayna. There is." He expelled a harsh breath. "You've been back for a week. I was hoping you would call me."

"Vince—"

"You're still upset with me," he supplied. "And I understand."

Surely he wasn't here to try to win her love again. And yet, Shayna feared that was exactly the case.

"These past two weeks without you in my life have seemed like a lifetime, Shayna. A lifetime without you. Every day I regret the stupid…" His voice trailed off, and he gritted his teeth. "Shayna, I still love you. I've never stopped."

Shayna held up a hand. "Vince—"

"No," Vince said, his voice low and husky as he stepped toward her. "Don't push me away, Shayna. Not until you've heard what I have to say."

Shayna stared at Vince, a man who just over two weeks ago she'd been planning to marry. And she realized that whatever he said wouldn't matter. Nothing he said would change how she felt.

"There's nothing to say, Vince."

"Yes, there is. At the wedding, you totally surprised me when you brought up the fact that you'd seen me with that stripper. And I reacted the way any guy would in that situation. I lied. I played down my responsibility, blamed it on alcohol. And that's why I'm here now, Shayna. To tell you that I was wrong not to be honest with you in the first place. You deserved my honesty if nothing else. And so I'm here to throw myself at your mercy and beg for your forgiveness."

Shayna continued to look at Vince, not saying anything. She wasn't sure what he expected her to say.

"I messed up, Shayna. And there's no excuse for what I did. Maybe it was a moment of panic, a second where I thought to myself, 'Oh, my God, I'm about to be married. Off the market.' I don't know. And ultimately, it doesn't matter. Nothing excuses my bad judgment. I'm just hoping that you can find it in your heart to forgive me. And to know that I would never, ever do anything like that again."

Something inside of Shayna twisted. Not because she was regretting the loss of her relationship with Vince but because it was so clear to her now that they weren't meant to be. She had felt more passion and desire for Donovan in their short time together than she had ever felt for Vince.

That wasn't to say that had she and Vince gotten married

she wouldn't have been the wife he needed her and wanted her to be. But in the wake of all that had happened, both the night before their wedding and since, she knew without a doubt that there was no going back.

Having met Donovan, even if their relationship never worked out as she feared it wouldn't, she knew she could never settle. Settle for a man who cheated on her. For one she didn't feel a crazy sense of passion for.

Vince stepped toward her, closing the last of the distance between them. And when he snaked his arms around her waist, Shayna didn't pull away.

There should have been some feeling of love or angst or even hatred. But instead, she felt nothing. No stirring of anything.

Vince lowered his head and pressed his lips against her cheek. And that's when Shayna pulled back, easing out of his arms.

"Shayna… Baby, please. Two weeks without you is punishment enough. And trust me, I've learned my lesson. I'm feeling so bad about what I've done—"

"Vince, stop," Shayna said firmly, taking several steps away from him. "What happened it doesn't matter anymore."

Vince's lips erupted in a grin. "Oh, Shayna. You don't know how happy that makes me. How happy I am to hear that you're ready to move beyond the past."

"Yes, I am," Shayna said, realizing Vince had misconstrued her words. "But not in the way you think," she began slowly, knowing this was going to hurt Vince but knowing that he was ultimately the one who had hurt himself. "Vince, I can't ever be with you again. There's no going back to the life we had after what happened."

Vince's face fell. "What?"

"It's over, Vince."

He looked confused. "I'm laying my heart on the line here,

Shayna. Telling you that I was the biggest fool in the world to do what I did. That I need you. I'm not expecting you to forgive me today. I know it will take time. But all I wanted you to say is that you'll give me that chance. Give me the chance to earn your love again."

Vince reached for her cheek, softly stroking it with his finger. "If you ever loved me, Shayna, I know you can do that. Give me that second chance to prove to you I'll be the man you need."

Shayna swallowed. She thought of the time she'd spent with Donovan, of the explosive passion, of that easy rapport, and she knew that what she would say next would possibly devastate Vince. But there was no getting around it.

"That's just it, Vince," Shayna said faintly. "I don't think you'll ever be the man I need. Maybe…maybe I never really loved you the way a woman is supposed to love a man."

"What?" Vince asked, his voice tinged with surprise. And maybe something else.

"I don't mean that I never loved you," Shayna quickly said. "But somewhere along the way, we lost something in our relationship. Or maybe we never really had it. That crazy passion two people should have when they're in love."

"We had that," Vince said, a definite hard edge to his voice now. "You know we had passion."

"I'm not speaking about our time in the bedroom," Shayna said. Although, if she were completely honest with herself, she had to admit that what she and Vince shared didn't even come close to what she and Donovan did in that regard. "I'm speaking in general. I just wonder now—especially given what you did—if what we had was enough. Because the man I want to spend my life with is a man who will never, even if he could get away with it, even if he could excuse it with alcohol or medication, *ever* cheat on me."

"Like I said," Vince said, no longer sounding like the meek

man wanting his fiancée's forgiveness, "I was stupid. I'm a man, Shayna. We can be weak at times. You can't expect a guy to be perfect."

"I don't expect perfection," Shayna said. "But I do believe that a man who is totally and completely in love with a woman will never hurt her the way you hurt me."

Vince had been regarding her with a baffled expression, but suddenly his eyes widened and he nodded his head, as though something had just become clear to him. "Ah, I get it. You met someone else."

Shayna's stomach lurched. Was it obvious, or was he guessing? Because she hadn't expected him to say that. She hadn't expected him to even suspect it.

"That's it," Vince said, actually chuckling. "So you went to Jamaica by yourself and found some guy to lick your wounds." His chest rose and fell with a heavy breath, and suddenly he wasn't chuckling anymore. "All right. I can't say I didn't deserve that."

"Nothing that happened in Jamaica had anything to do with you," Shayna interjected.

"So something *did* happen in Jamaica?"

"I didn't say that."

"You may as well have."

Shayna crossed her arms over her chest. "Will you please leave?"

"So it's true," Vince said, nodding his head. "You had an affair."

Shayna exhaled sharply and decided there was no point in hiding what had happened. "It wasn't an affair. I met someone who was nice—"

"Someone you could use to get back at me," Vince retorted.

"It had nothing to do with you. I fell for him because he's the complete opposite of you. A total gentleman who would never hurt a woman the way you hurt me. A man who I could tell, right from the beginning, had a sense of integrity that would never waiver."

"Right," Vince said sarcastically. "I'll bet that's what you were able to figure out. In how long? A day? Two? Is that how long it took for him to get into your pants?" The anger was evident on his face. "How long did it take for my fiancée—"

"None of your damn business!"

"I can't believe you. You get on my case for cheating—"

"Because that's what you did, Vince! *You* cheated on me. I was a single woman when I went to Jamaica. One with a broken heart because of what *you* did to me. But now—" She stopped herself from completing the thought.

Because it was absurd.

Certainly she was not in love with Donovan.

And yet when she thought of him, especially as compared to Vince, he had everything she wanted in a perfect man. The passion she'd described to Vince, the chemistry, the commitment.

The integrity.

"You slept with someone else days after you were supposed to marry me," Vince said accusingly. "Were you sober? Or were you drunk?"

"I'm not going to answer that question," Shayna said. "I owe you no explanation."

The intense look of anger on Vince's face startled her. Scared her, even. And then it made her mad. Because he didn't have the right.

"I want you to leave," Shayna told him. "I have nothing else to say to you."

Vince stared at her a moment longer, as if hoping she'd wither under his glare. When she didn't, he glanced away and loudly sighed. Then he turned back to her and said, "I'm shocked, Shayna. I didn't expect it."

"Didn't expect me to move on?" Shayna asked. "You thought I would pine away for you for the rest of my life?"

"That's not what I was going to say," Vince said. "I didn't expect you to meet someone, or to…do whatever you did. But I forgive you." His eyes met and held hers. "I forgive you because I love you. And I still believe you love me. You were so hurt because of what I did that you had to find someone else to sleep with. To fill that void. I get it. I don't like it—but I get it. And I know that someday soon you'll be able to see this whole situation with perspective and you'll come back to me."

Shayna almost felt sorry for Vince. Almost. But if he had loved her so much how had he ended up in the backseat of his car with a *stripper?* That was a question for which he would never be able to give her an answer that she could forgive.

Besides, she had moved on.

"Vince, please. Please leave now. I really don't want to be having this conversation."

Vince nodded and then smiled softly. "All right, but remember what I said. I'm going to wait for you, as long as it takes. Because I love you."

Vince left, and Shayna quickly locked the door behind him. With him gone, she leaned her back against the door and exhaled the anxious breath she'd kept inside.

What had just happened was almost unbelievable. Vince had done what she would have preferred he do in the first place—completely accept responsibility for his actions without any lame excuses. But it no longer mattered.

Because she truly had moved on.

Another man was in her heart.

Another man it was unlikely she would ever have a relationship with.

And unlike the ease with which she'd gotten over Vince, Shayna knew that getting over Donovan would be a lot harder.

Chapter 20

Vince e-mailed Shayna no less than once a day for the rest of the week, alternately begging for forgiveness and expressing his dismay over the fact that clearly she had never loved him. Shayna hadn't responded once, and if he continued to e-mail her, she vowed to block his e-mail address.

Perhaps what bothered her more than the messages was the fact that his words had gotten to her on some level. How *had* she so easily fallen for another man when she was supposed to be in love with Vince? The more she'd thought about that question as the week went on, the more she'd come to mistrust the feelings she believed she'd come to have for Donovan in such a short time.

And she was pretty certain that Donovan had come to the same conclusion, as well.

Because he hadn't called or e-mailed.

Shayna had spoken to some of her friends about her affair, and they'd all come to the same conclusion—she had had a rebound fling and that sort of relationship was destined to crash and burn.

"I would avoid all contact with him," her friend Cheryl had added. "Talking to him will only help perpetuate the false belief that you'll actually be able to develop a relationship. Trust me, you can try—but it's unlikely it will last."

Again, Shayna's heart and brain were at odds. Because her heart didn't want to believe that what she had shared with Donovan was a meaningless fling. But her brain believed that her friends were right. Especially Cheryl, who had gone through such an island relationship herself, only to end up crushed.

Shayna vowed to put Donovan out of her mind but found the task all but impossible. On Friday, she decided to send him a short e-mail, asking if she could have an address where she could send his sister an autographed book because she had promised her one.

Again, Donovan hadn't replied.

And Shayna was left with the feeling that her friends were right.

The next day during her book signing at the Borders Express at the Boulevard Mall, Shayna looked up—and promptly felt a spasm of shock.

Was that *Audrey* at the back of the crowd around her table? Donovan's sister?

She stared at the woman, her heart pounding wildly. And in the next instant, she knew that it *was* Audrey. Because behind her stood Donovan.

His eyes met hers from the back of the crowd.

And then he smiled.

Donovan saw the moment when Shayna saw him. Her eyes widened, and her lips parted. She was surprised. This was probably the last place she had expected to see him. Especially since he hadn't responded to the e-mail she'd sent yesterday. He hadn't because he'd wanted to surprise her by showing up at her signing, which he had seen advertised on her Web site.

Shayna was noticeably flustered. She barely made eye contact with the woman who stood before her ready to get her book signed. She kept throwing surreptitious glances in his direction.

Donovan stood back with his hands in the front pockets of his jeans, casually observing Shayna in action. He'd never been to a book signing before. Though he'd witnessed his own sister's reaction to her, it was weird to see the throng of women surrounding her, excited to talk to her about her work. They went on about various characters in her stories as though they were real people.

The women here made it clear that Shayna was a beloved storyteller. And Donovan knew why. It was her gracious nature as well as the riveting stories she told. He had read *Storm of Passion* and had learned for himself the talent she had at putting words to paper.

After about ten minutes, Audrey finally reached Shayna. Donovan continued to hang at the back of the crowd. Shayna stood to greet his sister, giving Audrey a big hug. He wasn't quite close enough to hear what they were saying, but it was obvious that Audrey was gushing over her as she had in Jamaica.

Shayna met his gaze once more, holding it for a beat before looking away. With his sister at the table, he ventured closer. How he had missed her. All he wanted to do was take her away from this spot in the mall, gather her in his arms and lay a kiss on her she would not soon forget.

He would get his chance to do just that.

Soon.

* * *

Shayna's heart was beating so fast she thought it might implode. Seriously, the rate at which it was going could not be healthy.

"It is so good to see you!" Audrey said as she rocked Shayna back and forth in a warm hug.

Shayna glanced at Donovan, saw that he was continuing to stare at her with an intent gaze. Despite everything she'd told herself, the gaze warmed every part of her body.

A flash of the memory of when she and Donovan had been kissing in the falls filled her mind. That had been the moment she had known, without doubt, that they would end up in bed. The moment she knew that her attraction to him had taken on a life of its own.

But she tried to force the image out of her mind and concentrate on Audrey. "What are you doing here?"

"I came to get my books signed." Audrey lifted a tote bag she had rested on the floor onto the table. It probably held every book Shayna had written.

"You came all this way for that?"

"We wanted to surprise you." Audrey glanced over her shoulder at Donovan, then back at Shayna. "My brother really misses you."

Shayna stole another quick glimpse of Donovan before picking up her pen. She was surprised to hear that Donovan missed her. He hadn't sent her any e-mails, hadn't called. She was stunned that he and Audrey were here right now.

Not addressing the comment Audrey had made, Shayna asked, "Did you fly? Did you drive? Where are you staying?"

"We drove. And we're staying at the Adams Mark right downtown."

Shayna nodded, playing nonchalant. She knew the

downtown hotel very well. It was quite close to her home. "Would you like me to sign all of these books to you?"

"You'd better believe it," Audrey said, chuckling. "And once they're signed, I don't lend them out. Actually, I never lend your books out, anyway. I love them too much." She squealed. "Oh, I'm so excited!"

Shayna faithfully signed each and every book, putting a personalized message in only a few of them. There were still other women behind Audrey waiting to buy books.

Audrey thanked Shayna and then went to the side and joined her brother. Shayna noticed that Donovan had not joined them at the table and wondered why.

The minutes passed and she signed more books. At one point she noticed that Audrey was no longer there. But Donovan still was.

Finally, with the crowd mostly dwindled, he came to the table. He was holding a copy of *Storm of Passion*. The book was worn around the edges, indicating it had already been read. Perhaps even studied.

"Hello," Shayna said. She tried to sound casual, as though Donovan's sudden arrival hadn't thrown her for a loop.

"Hey," Donovan said. He looked at her with a quiet intensity.

"I'm really surprised to see you here," Shayna said.

"That was the plan." Donovan paused and slid his book across the table to her. "Will you sign this for me?"

"Of course."

Shayna had tried to tell herself that what she had shared with Donovan had ended the day they said goodbye. That she would soon forget him and move on. But seeing him now, it was clear that she had lied to herself.

She still felt an almost startling reaction to the man. Her body was thrumming with desire, and thoughts of getting naked with him were suddenly at the forefront of her mind.

"It looks like you've read this already," Shayna said.

Donovan nodded. "I did."

"And?" Shayna closed her eyes, preparing for his review of her work. She always feared people telling her they didn't like her books. With Donovan in particular, she was even more concerned about his opinion.

"And it was very good," Donovan said. "Excellent, in fact."

She blew out a relieved breath. "Really?"

"I loved it."

That meant a lot to her. Maybe more than it should have. "Are you surprised you enjoyed it?"

"No, I'm not surprised. You're a passionate person. You can tell that in your writing."

Shayna flushed hotly, then looked beyond Donovan's shoulder to see if the woman standing there had overheard what he'd said. Donovan quickly looked over his shoulder, too, then scooped up another of Shayna's books and stepped to the side.

Holding the pen over the title page, Shayna considered the words she would write to Donovan. In the end, she chose: *I truly enjoyed the time we spent together. I will treasure it always.*

Pushing the book in Donovan's direction, Shayna smiled brightly at the woman who had picked up *Storm of Passion,* trying to feign a calmness she didn't feel. The woman had Shayna sign the book for her, then went into the store to pay for it.

And then it was just Shayna and Donovan again.

She was nervous as she regarded him, wanting to keep the feelings she had for him suppressed.

"I sent you an e-mail yesterday," she told him.

"I know."

"You didn't respond."

"Because I wanted to surprise you by showing up today." He paused. "Are you?"

"Very."

The bookseller came to the table and announced that the time for her signing was up. Shayna signed several copies of the books, then gathered her belongings.

"Where's your sister?" she asked.

"She left so we could talk."

"As in left the mall?"

"I'm not sure where she is. Probably shopping. I'll call when I'm ready. Though I was hoping…"

His voice trailed off, and he simply stared at her.

"Hoping what?" Shayna asked.

"That you might want to spend some time with me, maybe get something to eat."

Shayna was happy to see Donovan—she was—and yet… She felt out of sorts.

"Donovan, you know I told you we should wait two months before…before seeing if there's still something between us."

"You think I want to sleep with you?" he asked.

She shrugged. If she spent time with him, she was certain that they'd end up in bed.

Shayna began to walk, and Donovan walked with her.

"I came because I wanted to see you, Shayna. Because I missed you. I was hoping you'd be happy to see me."

"It's not that I'm not happy to see you…"

"Then what is it?"

"It's that I'm feeling pressured," she admitted. Maybe it was all that had happened with Vince this week and her subsequent questioning of what she'd shared with Donovan.

"I'm not trying to pressure you," he told her. "Not at all."

"Then why didn't you give me some warning?" she countered. "Instead, you show up like this—"

Donovan abruptly moved in front of her, taking her by her upper arms. "If you don't want to see me, just say so."

It wasn't that she didn't want to see him, and yet she couldn't tell him that. And she realized why.

Because she was afraid. Afraid that she was going to end up hurt by him.

"It's not that I don't want to see you," she began. "It's that I told you I needed time. I just…I just want you to respect that."

Donovan's jaw tightened. He was upset. Shayna should have said something to make him feel better, yet she was unable to open her mouth and do so.

She kept thinking about the e-mails from Vince, where he'd called her flaky for falling out of love and into love so quickly.

Her brain knew that Vince was trying to get to her, to make her feel guilty. But still, the words had gotten to her.

"So this two months you want me to wait," Donovan began, "you think that's the amount of time it's going to take to realize that the feelings we developed are real?"

"Yes," Shayna said, but she didn't really believe it.

"So I came all this way and you want me to leave? Without spending any time with you?"

"I don't want to be pressured. By you or by anybody."

Again, her words seemed to have hurt him. Donovan nodded. "Wow. Well, the last thing I want to do is *pressure* you by assuring you I'm still interested. So why don't we do this—you call me when two months is up. Or whenever it is you feel is an appropriate amount of time."

"Donovan…" Shayna began, but stopped. She *was* out of sorts. She felt snippy and irritated. And in her heart, she knew it wasn't really Donovan's fault. It was her own fear. Fear fueled by her friends' comments and her own insecurity.

He held up a hand. "It's okay."

"I'm still interested in—"

"Yeah, that's obvious."

Now Shayna was the one who felt crushed.

"Look, Donovan." She sighed. "I'll be honest with you. I've talked to some people close to me, and they're convinced that what happened between us was simply a rebound thing. I'm not saying I believe that, but is it wrong for me to want time to make sure that's not the case?"

"So you're letting what people say affect how you feel?"

"These things happen, Donovan. People hook up on vacation, and it ends up leading nowhere. It happened to a good friend of mine. I don't want to be naive."

"I don't care what people say," Donovan told her. "I don't care that people might believe it impossible to fall in love with someone in just a few days. I know otherwise—because I fell in love with you."

God, the words made her heart fill with hope. She wanted to believe him. Very much. "Donovan—"

"Shh." He placed his palm on her face, and Shayna exhaled a shuddery breath at his warm touch. Memories of Jamaica flooded her mind. "Why can't you trust what you're feeling?"

"Because…because I don't want to be wrong."

"You won't be. Trust me. I know what I feel. And I believe you feel the exact same thing. That's why I came all the way here, Shayna. Tell me you feel nothing for me."

Shayna thought Donovan might kiss her, right here in this crowded mall, if for no other reason than to prove his words true. She wanted him to.

But she said, "I just need more time. Time to be alone and figure out what I really feel."

Donovan raised his other hand to her face and stared into her eyes. It was as if he was looking into her soul.

Shayna's breathing became ragged. Was he going to kiss

her? Lord, how a big part of her wanted to throw her arms around his neck and lay one on him, throwing all caution to the wind. To believe that Donovan was right, not her friends.

"I believe in saying what you want, Shayna. So I'm going to say this. I know I want you. I'm not going to question why I feel the way for you that I do. Because you know what? I've waited a long time to feel this way for a woman again. And now I do."

He held her face, gazing into her eyes. Shayna wanted to tell him what she knew he wanted to hear. But she was confused. Her friends had told her that she'd jumped from one relationship to another, and they'd been right. They'd added that she needed time to be on her own to truly be certain of her feelings.

"If what we feel for each other is real," Shayna began slowly, "we'll still feel it six weeks from now."

Donovan lowered his hands and drew in an audible breath. "Sorry. I shouldn't have touched you. I forgot what you said about *pressure*."

"Please don't leave angrily. This isn't easy for me."

"All right." A definite look of disappointment filled Donovan's eyes. "You want time, you take the time you need. But remember, Shayna—sometimes all a person has is right now. This moment."

With that, he turned and walked away. He didn't glance back.

Shayna steeled her spine, tried to watch him go without any emotion. This was the way it had to be.

And yet, as he disappeared into the crowd, something inside of her collapsed.

Had she just pushed away her Mr. Right?

Chapter 21

Shayna could not deny that she was depressed for the next few days. She kept replaying in her mind the way Donovan had walked away from her.

She wanted to call him. But she knew that to call him, especially after having given him the two-month timetable, wouldn't be fair to him. It would be like dangling a carrot in front of a horse and wondering why the horse got frustrated if the carrot was pulled away.

No, she had resolved to avoid contact with him for the next six weeks.

She was grateful that she had figured out a new historical idea. On Tuesday, she was busy trying to plot her new novel when the phone rang. She ran to answer it, glancing at the caller ID first.

It was her mother.

"Hey, Mom," Shayna said cheerfully when she picked up the phone.

"Hi, baby. How are you?"

"I'm good."

"Are you?"

"Yeah. Sure. Getting back into the swing of things. I've finally got an idea for the next book."

"Well, that's good to hear." Her mother paused, and Shayna felt there was something else she wanted to say. "Honey, how are you feeling about…things with Vince?"

"I'm feeling the same as I did before I left for Jamaica. That it's over."

Shayna's mother sighed wearily. "Oh, sweetheart. I'm sorry to hear that."

"Why?"

"Because…because I believe that everyone makes mistakes, and we're all deserving of forgiveness."

"Mom, he *cheated* on me the night before our wedding. And it wasn't like he fell into bed with an old friend. He slept with a stripper. That's unforgivable."

"He came by earlier," Alice said. "Wanted to talk about you."

Oh, heck, Shayna thought. Vince had failed to get through to her, so he had gone to speak to her parents to get them to influence her decision about forgiving him?

"He came to see me, too," Shayna said. "Last week."

"Yes, he mentioned that. He said he was hoping he would have heard from you by now."

Shayna laughed without mirth. "I made it clear I wouldn't be calling him."

"I know, sweetheart. But he loves you. You can't blame him for trying."

"Mom—"

"Sometimes, Shayna, there is no reward for being so rigid in one's belief. As I said before—we all need forgiveness. No one's perfect. Not even you."

Alarm bells went off in Shayna's head. She had a sinking

feeling in her gut that she knew what Vince had told her mother. Which meant that she'd been wrong in her assumption about why he'd visited her parents. He hadn't been interested in getting their help in winning her back.

He wanted to out her.

"Whatever he told you—"

"I'm going to reserve judgment," her mother said. "I know that in your right frame of mind you never would have begun an affair with a man you barely know. But Vince broke your heart, and you were hurting."

Shayna was flabbergasted. "I can't believe Vince told you that! He had no right to—"

"He loves you," Shayna's mother interjected. "He made a horrible mistake, but now he's not the only one."

"You think I made a mistake?" Shayna said, a tad defensively.

"An affair like this—yes, women do tend to regret them. You let a man you barely knew sweet-talk you into his bed. I'm sure he was very convincing. Just as I'm sure you were probably not the first woman he did this to. Men are good at seeing vulnerable women and taking advantage of them."

Shayna hadn't planned to discuss this with her mother, but now she had no choice. "He didn't take advantage of me."

"I'm sure you don't want to believe that—"

"He *didn't*," Shayna insisted. "And I don't regret the time I spent with him. He's far more a man than Vince will ever be."

"Oh, sweetheart. You don't really believe that."

"I do believe it—because it's true. Donovan was a complete gentleman. He was sweet and charming, and because of him, I had a vacation I'll never forget."

"Donovan?" her mother asked. "That's his name?"

"Yes. His name is Donovan Deval, and he's from Maryland. He's the owner of a few clothing stores."

"You're not planning to see him again?" Alice Kenyon couldn't have sounded more shocked.

"What if I were?" Shayna asked.

"Oh, for goodness' sake. What would come of it?"

"He's a nice man. Respectful. Caring."

"Oh, Shayna. Please tell me you haven't developed feelings for him."

"Is it impossible that I could have met someone I like? Someone I'm interested in getting to know better?"

"When just three weeks ago, you were in love with Vince?"

It was a rhetorical question, and Shayna didn't answer it.

"Please don't delude yourself, Shayna. This man—he saw that you were vulnerable—"

"He didn't take advantage of me, Mom."

"Okay, let's say he didn't. The fact remains that you were in love with someone else for close to two years. You're angry with Vince now, and any feelings you might have for Donovan are based in vengeance."

"Vengeance?"

"Yes, sweetheart. Please don't let yourself believe that you can successfully start a relationship with someone after knowing him for a week."

"I guess you should date someone for a solid year and a half first, right?" Shayna asked, unable to keep the sarcasm from her voice. "Date him for that long and even plan a wedding. That'll ensure a man will love you forever, never cheat on you."

Shayna's mother didn't say a word. Her comment had hit home.

With her mother—and with her.

Dating someone for a long time didn't guarantee a relationship would last. And who was to say that because you didn't know someone for a certain amount of months or years that it meant your relationship was doomed to fail?

"Oh, my God."

"What is it, Shayna?" her mother asked.

"I've been so stupid," Shayna muttered.

Shayna thought she heard her mother say something along the lines of "It's okay, you just made a mistake." And she realized her mother must've misunderstood her comment. But she didn't bother to respond to that. All she could think about was the mistake she'd made in pushing Donovan away.

She had pushed away the one man in her life she'd felt an inexplicable chemistry to because she'd bought into the fact that they hadn't known each other long enough to have a fighting chance.

The truth was, she'd known him long enough to know that he was everything a good man should be. And just as importantly, she knew that she was attracted to him and he to her. They'd connected on a level beyond the physical. She'd felt it again when he'd shown up at her book signing on Saturday, but she'd been so damn stubborn—or, as her mother had said, rigid.

Yes, she'd been too rigid to see that what her friends might have experienced or believed didn't necessarily apply to what she had experienced with Donovan.

"I have to go, Mom."

"Sweetheart—"

"I'll call you later, okay?"

Shayna quickly hung up, not giving her mother a chance to respond.

It was all so clear to her now. She was pushing Donovan away because she felt their relationship couldn't possibly last given that she'd only known him for a week. And yes, she'd also been afraid of getting hurt. That had been a big part of her concern.

But there were no guarantees in life. She had learned that lesson the hard way.

So had Donovan.

She missed him. No matter how much she'd tried to stop thinking about him, she couldn't. What was the point in waiting six more weeks to be certain of what she felt when her heart knew that in that time nothing would change?

Shayna found her cell phone and punched in the number for Donovan. The phone rang four times and went to voice mail.

She left a message. Then she sent him an e-mail, telling him simply that she missed him and wanted to talk.

And then she waited.

Donovan didn't call. And he didn't e-mail her. Two days later, Shayna was beginning to feel she'd ruined things for good.

But early Thursday afternoon, a call came in on her cell phone with a 301 area code. Grinning from ear to ear, she pressed Talk.

"Hello?"

"Shayna?"

She frowned. It was a woman's voice, not a man's. "Yes?"

"Oh, thank God. I'm so glad I reached you."

The person on the other end of the line sounded like she'd been crying. And she sounded a bit like...

"Audrey?" Shayna asked.

"Yes, Shayna." More sniffling. "It's me."

"Audrey, what's wrong?" Shayna asked.

"It's Donovan."

A cold chill raced down Shayna's arms. "Oh, my God. Something's happened to him." She knew it, could hear it in Audrey's voice.

"He would be so angry with me for calling you."

"Audrey, what happened to Donovan?"

"He was in the store. Closing up. And…" Audrey stopped, drew in an unsteady breath.

"And what?" Shayna all but shrieked, completely panicked.

"They shot him." Audrey began to cry. "Oh, God."

"What?" Shayna's limbs went numb. "He's—he's—" *Please, God, no…*

"He's in the hospital. In critical condition. He's been in a coma for the last couple of days."

"Couple of days?"

"Yes. He was shot on Tuesday."

The very day she had finally called him. The tragic irony wasn't lost on her.

"It was touch and go for a while, but the doctors think he's gonna pull through."

"Is he still in a coma?"

"Yes. We keep praying he wakes up soon."

"Which hospital?"

"Laurel Regional Hospital," Audrey replied.

Shayna's mind was whirling. Either she could get in her car and drive, or she could head to the airport and catch a flight.

"I'm on my way," Shayna said. "Is the number on my phone the one where I can reach you?"

"Yes. Oh, Shayna. I'm glad you're coming. I think…I think it'll help."

"I'll be there by this evening," Shayna said. "I'll call you later, okay?"

She hung up and began to scramble around her apartment. She needed a suitcase. She needed some clothes.

Hurrying to her closet, she found the suitcase she'd taken

with her to Jamaica. And just seeing it sent her over the edge.

Remembering the wonderful time she'd had with Donovan, she suddenly feared she would never kiss him again. Never see that sexy smile again.

Never make love to him again.

She began to cry. The last words Donovan had said to her before he'd walked away from her in the mall hit her with full force.

Sometimes, all a person has is right now. This moment.

"Oh, God." She clutched her stomach. "Please let Donovan be okay. Please don't let the last time I saw him be all we'll ever have."

The tears streamed down her cheeks now.

She wanted more time with Donovan.

She wanted a life with him.

But was it too late?

Shayna ended up checking flights online and found that a flight was due to leave in just about two hours. She quickly packed some clothes in her small suitcase and raced to the airport.

Shortly after four, she touched down at BWI. Wasting no time, she rented a car—then promptly hit the road to head to Laurel, Maryland.

Donovan's last words continued to haunt her. All she kept thinking as she drove was *Lord, don't let it be too late.*

By five, she was pulling into the parking lot at the hospital. She called Audrey as she parked, and by the time she entered the hospital doors, Audrey was there, waiting for her.

The two women embraced, and Shayna began to cry again. "How's he doing?" Shayna asked.

"He's awake," Audrey said, grinning through her tears. "He woke up about half an hour ago."

"Oh, thank God." Waves of relief washed over Shayna. "Can I see him?"

Audrey nodded. "Yes. It's supposed to be just family, but I told the nurse staff that his fiancée was arriving."

"Does he know I'm…I'm coming?"

Audrey shook her head. "I didn't tell him. After we left Buffalo, he told me what you'd said…that you wanted space. So I knew he would tell me not to call you. But I did anyway."

"I'm glad you did," Shayna said. She deeply regretted their last conversation, how she'd foolishly pushed Donovan away. "Now, please—take me to Donovan."

A short while later, Shayna was upstairs, outside of Donovan's room. The family members she'd met in Jamaica were there, as well as his mother and others. They all greeted her warmly, as though she was already a member of the family.

They accepted her instantly, which brought more tears to her eyes. How had she ever, for a moment, believed that what she and Donovan had shared wasn't real?

Donovan's brother exited the hospital room with Lynda, and seeing her, they both smiled. Again, they greeted her with warm hugs.

Then Shayna opened the door and entered Donovan's room.

At the very first sight of him, emotion overwhelmed her. Lord, he looked frail. He had an IV in his arm and a bandage across his forehead.

Shayna stepped farther into the room. His eyes were closed, and she wondered if he'd fallen asleep.

She would sit with him nonetheless. Talk to him.

As she approached the bed, his eyes suddenly opened. Then widened as they settled on her.

"Yes, Donovan," she began, her voice cracking. "It's me. Shayna."

His eyes narrowed, as though he didn't believe what he was seeing.

"I'm really here. You're not dreaming."

"Shayna…"

He lifted his hand, the one attached to the IV. Shayna hurried to the bed and took it gently between both of her own. "You don't have to say anything, Donovan. Just know that I'm here with you."

"How?" he asked. His voice was hoarse.

"Audrey called me."

"But it's not…two months."

Her ridiculous two-month requirement. "Please, don't mention anything about that." She kissed his thumb. "This isn't the time."

"No?"

She shook her head. "No."

Silence passed between them. Then Donovan said, "Why did you come?"

"Because the moment I heard, I knew I had to get to you."

Donovan closed his eyes, and at least a minute passed with neither of them saying anything. Shayna knew he needed his rest. She was content to sit with him and hold his hand.

But Donovan suddenly opened his eyes again, and asked, "Are you here because you feel sorry for me?"

"No," Shayna said, shaking her head. "Absolutely not."

"Then why?"

"Shh," Shayna cooed. "Donovan, get your rest. We can talk about everything later."

"Tell me," he said slowly. "Tell me what you want."

He had to know what she wanted. She was here—by his side.

I believe in saying what I want. His words when she'd last seen him in Buffalo sounded in her mind.

"I want you, Donovan." She pressed his palm against her cheek, tears filling her eyes. "I realized that before your sister called me to tell me what…what happened to you. I want you to know that. I'm not just here because of her call. On Tuesday, I realized that my pushing you away made no sense. I let my fear keep me from believing that what we had was real. I called you that day, e-mailed you. But I didn't reach you. Now…" Her voice cracked. "Now I know why."

She was crying now, unable to hold her emotion back.

"Baby…"

"All the way here, I kept thinking about what you said. That sometimes, all you have with a person is that moment when you're with them. That you never know if you'll have tomorrow. And I feel so stupid for pushing you away."

"It's okay," Donovan said softly.

"I want you, Donovan. Only you. And I almost lost you…"

"Shh." This time, Donovan was the one to offer her comfort. "The past doesn't matter. What matters is right now. And you're here."

"Oh, Donovan." He could have been angry with her, unwilling to give her another chance. But instead, he was embracing her with open arms. "I love you. I fell in love with you in Jamaica. I just didn't believe it could be true. But I know now that I did. And I promise I'll never let you go again."

Donovan smiled that charming, sexy smile, and Shayna's heart filled with hope.

And with love. All the love she had for this man who had completely captured her heart.

"I want to kiss you," he said, his voice raspy.

And despite where they were and the fact that he was

injured, Shayna's body grew warm. And she knew, without a doubt, that they had the kind of passion that drew two people together—and kept them deeply in love.

She leaned forward and kissed Donovan. Kissed him softly so as not to injure him. But their burning passion simmered even in the soft kiss.

The way it burned in their hearts.

Epilogue

Six months later, at the Gran Bahia Principe resort in Jamaica, Donovan and Shayna held hands beneath the gazebo on the beach. She was dressed in a simple white dress. He wore a white suit with a shirt that was open at the collar. Neither could stop grinning as they gazed into each other's eyes.

The sun was shining, and a breeze helped cool the otherwise hot day. The setting could not have been more picturesque.

Almost every chair in the gazebo was filled with wedding guests, people who had come to Jamaica to witness two people exchange vows of love.

Shayna glanced at the front row, where her parents sat. Her mother caught her eye—and smiled.

It had warmed Shayna's heart to no end that her mother had come around, accepting Donovan without any reservations. The way his family had accepted her. Her mother had gotten to know him and had no doubts that Donovan deeply loved her daughter.

Shayna then gazed to her right, where her sister once again

stood as her maid of honor. Brianne nodded, acknowledging that this time Shayna was marrying the right man.

And as Shayna glanced at the minister, she remembered that day seven months earlier when she'd been about to marry Vince.

But unlike that day, there were no regrets this time. No huge dark clouds of despair hanging over her head.

Today, everything was perfect.

Though she'd been horribly distressed on her wedding day seven months earlier, she was now eternally grateful that Vince had betrayed her. Because he had freed her from marrying the wrong person.

He had freed her so that she could ultimately meet the man of her dreams.

Donovan had asked her that first week they'd met in Jamaica if she believed in fate, and at the time, she hadn't been sure that she truly did.

But now, without a doubt, she knew she believed.

Fate had brought Donovan into her life—the man she was meant to love for a lifetime.

And that's what she would do. From this day forward.

For the rest of her life.

She looked once again at the man of her dreams, saw the smile that had won her over. Her heart swelled with love.

Then the ceremony began.

And what had started as an island fantasy turned into happily ever after when the minister pronounced them husband and wife.

REQUEST YOUR FREE BOOKS!

2 FREE NOVELS
PLUS 2 *FREE GIFTS!*

KIMANI™
ROMANCE

Love's ultimate destination!

YES! Please send me 2 FREE Kimani™ Romance novels and my 2 FREE gifts (gifts are worth about $10). After receiving them, if I don't wish to receive any more books, I can return the shipping statement marked "cancel." If I don't cancel, I will receive 4 brand-new novels every month and be billed just $4.69 per book in the U.S. or $5.24 per book in Canada. That's a saving of over 20% off the cover price. It's quite a bargain! Shipping and handling is just 50¢ per book in the U.S. and 75¢ per book in Canada.* I understand that accepting the 2 free books and gifts places me under no obligation to buy anything. I can always return a shipment and cancel at any time. Even if I never buy another book from Kimani Press, the two free books and gifts are mine to keep forever.

168 XDN E4CA 368 XDN E4CM

Name	(PLEASE PRINT)

Address	Apt. #

City	State/Prov.	Zip/Postal Code

Signature (if under 18, a parent or guardian must sign)

Mail to **The Reader Service:**
IN U.S.A.: P.O. Box 1867, Buffalo, NY 14240-1867
IN CANADA: P.O. Box 609, Fort Erie, Ontario L2A 5X3

Not valid for current subscribers to Kimani Romance books.

Want to try two free books from another line?
Call 1-800-873-8635 or visit www.morefreebooks.com.

* Terms and prices subject to change without notice. Prices do not include applicable taxes. N.Y. residents add applicable sales tax. Canadian residents will be charged applicable provincial taxes and GST. Offer not valid in Quebec. This offer is limited to one order per household. All orders subject to approval. Credit or debit balances in a customer's account(s) may be offset by any other outstanding balance owed by or to the customer. Please allow 4 to 6 weeks for delivery. Offer available while quantities last.

Your Privacy: Kimani Press is committed to protecting your privacy. Our Privacy Policy is available online at www.eHarlequin.com or upon request from the Reader Service. From time to time we make our lists of customers available to reputable third parties who may have a product or service of interest to you. If you would prefer we not share your name and address, please check here. ☐

Help us get it right—We strive for accurate, respectful and relevant communications. To clarify or modify your communication preferences, visit us at www.ReaderService.com/consumerschoice.

KROM10

THE WESTMORELANDS

NEW YORK TIMES
bestselling author

BRENDA JACKSON

HOT WESTMORELAND NIGHTS

Ramsey Westmoreland knew better than to lust after the hired help. But Chloe, the new cook, was just so delectable. Though their affair was growing steamier, Chloe's motives became suspicious. And when he learned Chloe was carrying his child this Westmoreland Rancher had to choose between pride or duty.

Available March 2010 wherever books are sold.

Always Powerful, Passionate and Provocative.

SD73013